Thumbprint Mysteries

MURDER AT THE REUNION

BY

BARBARA STEINER

CB

CONTEMPORARY BOOKS

a division of NTC/CONTEMPORARY PUBLISHING GROUP
Lincolnwood, Illinois USA

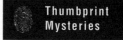

Thumbprint
Mysteries

MORE THUMBPRINT MYSTERIES

by Barbara Steiner:

The Party Boat Murders
Murder Takes a Fast Track

DEDICATION:
For Jim and Ann Short, with appreciation.

ACKNOWLEDGMENTS:
Thanks to Jim and Ann for my stay in their home on the lake, which became Jo's home. Also thanks to my critique group without whom the book wouldn't have been nearly so good: Kathleen, Regina, Jimmy, John C., John W. Any mistakes left are all mine. Also thanks to Linda Kwil, for her patience. And to Joan Lowery Nixon, who had the idea for this project.

Cover Design: Larry Didona

ISBN: 0-8092-0692-7

Published by Contemporary Books,
a division of NTC/Contemporary Publishing Group, Inc.,
4255 West Touhy Avenue,
Lincolnwood (Chicago), Illinois 60646-1975 U.S.A.
© 1998 Barbara Steiner

CHAPTER 1

Never go to your high school reunion. We'd heard the warnings. We swore we'd never darken the door of Hot Springs High once we escaped. But here we were, sitting in the parking lot. Not of the high school but, even worse, the parking lot of the country club.

Paka broke the silence. "We have special invitations, so we have to go through with this, but I don't know why we have to get together with people we went to high school with. We didn't party with them then. Why should we party with them now?"

"To see how the other half lives?" I asked.

"I like the way we live," Paka responded.

"I do too. But it won't hurt us to see what everyone else has been up to. Besides, sitting here dreading a party isn't making it go away. And don't forget, we're working. I'm supposed to write up the weekend parties for the newspaper."

"And I'm supposed to take photos."

"Then why *are* we sitting here?"

"I was waiting for you to get out. I'm not going in there by myself." Paka sighed and lifted her camera bag onto her lap. But she didn't get out of the car.

"We're much more successful now than we were in high school." I kept stalling.

"And we're beautiful." Paka turned to me and grinned. She *was* beautiful. We'd spent half our life savings on makeovers and new clothes at the mall in Little Rock. We both looked great.

"I still say the right side of your hair looks like a haystack."

Paka punched me. I laughed again and that got me moving.

I opened my door, pulled up my long skirt, and stepped out of my Nissan 4x4. The car was easy to get out of in tennis shoes, but a wobbly risk in high heels. I got my balance, took a deep breath of the cool, humid air, and listened to crickets chirping.

"I haven't worn high heels since graduation." Paka clunked along, her camera bag bumping her hip.

"Me either, and now I remember why. But this party will be a kick. After all, it's been ten years since we've seen some of these people."

"A hundred years wouldn't be long enough."

"How long since you've been to the country club?" I teased.

"Are you kidding?"

"The newspaper didn't *have* to give us a job," I said. "I would have gone out of curiosity."

"And you know who was killed by curiosity!"

"Meow!" I laughed. Paka laughed. We were in this

now for better or for worse.

Inside the door, two women sat at a table. One turned to me. "Jolene Allen. I'd have known you anywhere. You haven't changed a bit."

I took the name tag that Anilee Mowdy handed me, then looked down and wondered how to pin it to a dress with very little on the top.

"And Paka Powell. Hey, you look great. That pink sweater really suits you. I remember you wore black all the time in high school."

Paka bumped me with one hip as we walked away. "Sorry you wasted your two hundred bucks, Jolene. My money was well spent." She patted her poof of layered hair.

"Anilee's eyesight is going. I don't look anything like the short, chubby kid that everyone called Moon-Pie."

The beauty operator had streaked my mouse-brown hair with blonde. She had cut bangs that covered one side of my forehead, making my face look less round. She had lined and shadowed my eyes, making them look bigger and bluer. I thought I looked great.

I straightened my shoulders and yanked the top of my dress up a little. I marched into the ballroom where I could hear the party getting started. Paka was right beside me. I'd have to look up almost a foot to see the grin on her face. But I knew it was there.

We tapped our way straight to the bar. "I'll have a martini," Paka ordered.

I stared at her. "You've never drunk a martini before."

"I can't order a beer," she whispered. "A beer isn't sophisticated enough."

"You'll pass out. I need those photos."

"I'll just hold it. Pour it in a plant later."

"Could I get a Coke in one of those wineglasses?" I asked, pointing.

The bartender gave me a smile that said "recovering alcoholic." I didn't care what he thought. I wasn't, and I needed my head clear in order to write a story.

Paka and I have our own business. We graduated from high school, but neither of us wanted to go to college. Paka didn't have the money. My parents had a fit. But I knew how to write. I knew I'd learn everything else I needed on the job. And Paka was the best photographer ever to graduate from Hot Springs High School. Everyone said so.

She was the one who got a job at the *Sentinel Record*, Hot Springs' newspaper. She told them she wouldn't work without me because we'd been a team in high school. Fortunately, they took me on probation. I struggled for a few months, but I learn fast. I'm not dumb. I studied every story in the paper for weeks. I read some journalism books. I listened to my editor and learned from him.

To make a long story short, we became stars. And as soon as we had a little money saved, we quit the paper and formed our own business. We've just made our first sale to a national magazine.

"Look, there's Olen and Iva Nell." Paka pointed with her martini. I didn't tell her how impolite that was. When booze spilled down her hand, she licked off the dribble and took a sip. "Yuk. This tastes like kerosene."

"Told you."

We walked over to Olen Judd and his wife. Our big success was our article about them in *People* magazine. Olen is a director in Hollywood. His movies are low-budget, but not B films. They're intelligent science fiction stories. We were lucky. We'd called Olen and arranged to interview him and Iva Nell—she wrote the films. Then their new picture won an award at the Cannes Film Festival. *People* magazine snapped up my story and Paka's photos. Success is often a matter of being in the right place at the right time.

Olen whistled. "Look at you two. What happened? You look great."

Paka laughed. "You want to hit him, Jo, or shall I?"

Olen's face turned red. "I didn't mean— I—"

"It's okay, Olen," I said. "We know you didn't mean to hurt our feelings. And I'm glad to see you're the same short nerd you were before you hit the big time."

I'm five-four. Olen is only a couple of inches taller. I've always thought he was kind of cute. He has a head of thick, black curls that are usually out of control, even when cut short. Tonight he wore a tuxedo, his usual horn-rim glasses, and a big grin. Iva Nell had on a black dress that looked like a slip.

A couple, walking arm in arm, sauntered by and whisked Olen and Iva Nell away with them. "Hi, Jolene," the woman said.

Paka dumped her martini into the nearest fern, glass and all. She lifted her camera and snapped three photos.

"Notice that Corki didn't say, 'Hi, Paka'? I'm black, six feet tall without heels, and look absolutely gorgeous tonight. But I'm still invisible."

"So what's new, Pussycat?" I giggled.

Paka's name means "pussycat" in Swahili, but I know she can turn into a tiger. She was on her way now because of Corki's slight.

"She didn't mean to ignore you." I tried to explain Corki Meeler's behavior.

"Of course, she didn't. Let's get to work." Paka walked away, snapping photos as she went. I let her go. She'd cool off in a few minutes.

I took a big swig of Coke, turned around, and faced another couple.

"I'm so sorry about your parents, Jolene," the woman said. "My daddy always said that Senator Allen knew more about Arkansas politics than anybody else in this town. I know he'd have been re-elected."

"Thank you." Tears sprang to my eyes. I turned and walked away. I swallowed, trying to get past the wave of pain that washed over me.

My parents had both been killed in a car accident in April. They'd been driving home from Little Rock in a heavy rainstorm. The police said it looked like Daddy swerved to miss something on the road. Then he lost control of the car. It still doesn't take much for me to get emotional over my loss. And I still can't believe they're gone.

I leaned on the bar and breathed deeply a few times. Then I took a tiny notebook from my purse and concentrated on the party. When I turned around, I bumped into Ray Chronister. He acted and smelled as if he'd gotten started on the party earlier in the day.

"Hey, Jolene Allen. You still living out there on the lake in your daddy's house? Out there all alone?" Ray's face was red. Too much booze had made him older and fatter. He might be thirty, but he looked fifty. "If you need company some night, you let me know, you hear?" He grinned at me. I looked for an escape route.

The room had gotten crowded. People huddled in little clumps, laughing and talking. Remembering high school days, telling stories about each other. Some held out photos.

I knew they were talking about families—children. I didn't wish I was married or had kids. But I searched for Paka to wisecrack me out of the mood I had dropped into. I spotted her clear across the room.

I started a list of who was at the party. The couple who stole Olen and Iva Nell was Hank and Corki Meeler. Corki was in charge of the reunion weekend. I admired the way they looked together, the way they were obviously still madly in love.

Hank had been captain of the football team and president of the senior class. Corki was homecoming queen and prom queen. They were high school sweethearts. They went off to college together and then married right after graduation in a big Hot Springs society wedding.

Hank had put on a little weight, probably from eating with real estate clients. He and Anilee Mowdy owned the biggest real estate business in Hot Springs.

Corki was still a beauty. She was about five-four too, but she was slender. Her blonde hair was swept up on her head to make her look taller. She probably went to the beauty shop once a week, not once a year like I did. She was still a queen in Hot Springs society. Her picture was in the newspaper every other week for some charity ball or fund-raising event. I liked her. I couldn't believe she'd slighted Paka earlier, since she was nice to everyone.

"Having fun?" A woman stopped beside me. Betty Sue Trotter. She had dated Hank in high school and was staring at him now. I took a good look at her. She looked old and tired. If Hank ever saw her these days, he was probably glad he had dropped Betty Sue for Corki.

"I guess," I said. "Strange, isn't it? Ten years have gone by, but we take on the same image we had in high school."

"I've noticed that." Betty Sue smiled. "Corki is really happy, isn't she?"

"Yes, that's obvious."

"They have four children. Don't you want children, Jo?"

"Oh, some day—probably. Where's your husband?" I hoped I was right, that Betty Sue had married and was happy too—except that she didn't look happy.

"He's around here someplace. Talking football, I'm sure. I get awfully tired of football. You've done well with your life in ten years, Jo. Bet you travel a lot."

"We do," I said. "Paka and I take every job we're offered that means we get to go someplace."

"I'm going to get another drink. Want something?" Betty Sue turned to go.

"No, I've been nursing this Coke. Isn't there food around here someplace?"

"Over by the double doors to the dining room. Big buffet. Go check it out." She pointed and left, swaying a little. She didn't need another drink.

"Thanks, I will." I was glad to escape. Betty Sue's mood didn't help mine one bit.

I found Paka with the same idea—eating. "Get some good photos?" I asked her.

"Same-old, same-old. Not a very exciting party if you ask me. What we need is a rock and roll band. Get down and boogie." Paka did a little dance step.

"Eighties music was pretty bad, wasn't it?"

A live band played in one corner, but they couldn't compete with shrieks of laughter. Clinks of glasses. People's voices getting louder and louder as they relaxed.

"Think we could sneak out?" I said after we'd sampled the buffet and hung out for a little while. "If you have enough pictures, I can make up the rest of my story."

"You want to leave now? Didn't you hear that bang? Sounded like a gunshot, but I think someone is popping champagne corks."

"Since when have you become an authority on popping champagne corks?"

"Well, I've been to weddings. I hardly ever pop them myself, but— Hey, look!" Paka raised her camera. "Is that who I think it is? I want a photo. Where's she been?"

"She always did like to make an entrance, even if she had to be late to do so."

The woman who stopped beside us made us both look like giant lake creatures covered with muddy weeds.

"Venice?" I asked. "Venice Harwood? I didn't know you were back in town."

"Been here some time, Jo. How could you miss me?"

How, indeed. Venice was five-two, dark, exotic. Her hair was styled like a Thirties movie star. It waved from the part to cup around her face like a frame. What the hair framed was deep-set brown eyes, a tiny red mouth, and a pixie nose. What it didn't hide were ears like tiny shells. The lobes held the biggest diamond studs I'd ever seen—even in windows in Hot Springs jewelry shops. Were they real?

I knew I was staring. Paka helped me. "You went to New York and Hollywood too, didn't you, Venice? Why did you come back here?"

Venice looked at the martini in her hand. "Yes, I went both places. But I'll have to admit, I wasn't successful. Because I was a star in high school plays, I thought breaking into theater or the movies would be easy. It wasn't. I got discouraged and came home. I feel a lot safer here. I never felt safe in New York City or L.A."

"You tried." I didn't know what else to say. At least Venice was honest about what had happened. She didn't whine. She didn't make excuses. "If you hadn't tried, you'd have always wondered if you could have been a movie star."

"That's right. I read your magazine stories all the time, Jo. They're good. And you had a story in *People* magazine recently. That's great."

"We did." I included Paka. "I think they bought the piece because of Paka's photos."

"Your pictures are great, too, Paka. I didn't mean to overlook your work." There was a note of sadness in Venice's voice. I had never envied her, even in high school. Now I felt a little sorry for her. "You married?" I asked, to keep the conversation going.

"My husband's a jockey. Not a very successful jockey, I have to admit. I work at the track during the season, sell tickets."

"Oh. That must be interesting," I said. What a lame word—interesting.

"It is." She stood up straighter and walked away. "See you."

"I'm feeling a lot of woe here tonight, girl." Paka turned to me. "Sadness and woe. Someone should ban high school reunions."

"It must be sad to be a has-been before you're thirty. You know, Paka, I've always wondered if people who were stars in high school regret it. Especially if that's all they have the rest of their lives. They're never stars again. High school only lasts four years."

"There's a story here, Jo."

"But do I want to write it?"

Suddenly, the idea of writing anything flew right out of my mind. Paka and I both froze in time, real time—not the past—not high school days.

Screams echoed across the ballroom. Party noises turned into a dead silence.

CHAPTER 2

Paka almost dropped her camera. "My God, what's happening? Did someone break a fingernail?" Paka could be irreverent and funny any time of the day or night. She could find something humorous about almost any situation.

I had a bad feeling that this wasn't funny. The screams had contained an element of real pain and horror. "I think this might be more serious, Paka. Come on. Bring your camera." I took off running across the ballroom, where people stood frozen in little groups.

The screams came from the direction of the coatroom. I headed that way with Paka right behind me. People stepped out of our way, probably glad to see someone doing something. I didn't have any plan until I found out what was wrong, but the number one character trait for journalists is curiosity. I had worked at the newspaper long enough to smell a story, even one I might not like.

I slipped through the couples crowding the coatroom door. Corki Meeler cradled Hank, hugging him to her breast. She looked up at me, her face a mask of disbelief and horror.

I knelt beside her. "What's the matter, Corki?"

I had always thought that Hank Meeler was a candidate for a heart attack. His complexion was unnaturally red, and he was overweight. His father, young at the time, had died of a heart attack when we were in high school.

I looked around at a dozen curious faces. "Has anyone called a doctor?"

"Oh, Jo, it's too late," Corki sobbed. "Hank's dead."

She let Hank lie back on the floor. Her dress was smeared with blood. Hank's chest had a red stain that had spread to cover most of his upper body.

"Dead?"

Corki became very calm. Shock was taking over. "I sent him to get my jacket. It's early, but I was tired from all the work we've done to get the reunion organized, to do the planning for the party and the tours and—" She stopped talking, stared at Hank again, and started to cry softly.

I pulled her to her feet. She crumpled into my arms. "Oh, Jo, who would hurt Hank?"

I comforted Corki but looked back at the man on the floor. I hadn't seen many gunshot wounds, but it doesn't take a homicide detective to recognize a small hole in the center of a huge bloodstain.

"The police will call a photographer, Paka," I whispered. "But take several photos right now." I moved Corki out of the small room. Some air would help her immediate state. Someone needed to keep people out of the coatroom. I had worked on the newspaper long enough to know that it doesn't take much to contaminate a crime scene. I looked around for someone to take charge until a policeman did come.

"Jo, what's happened?" Anilee Mowdy had pushed through the growing crowd. "What's wrong with Corki?"

"Anilee, would you take Corki away from here and let her sit down? Hank's been shot. Give her some water or something stronger to drink. The rest of you move back. Don't anyone go into the coatroom. Here, you." I pointed to a high school-age girl I figured might have been working at the coatroom desk.

"Me?" She looked scared. I guessed she hadn't been at her post.

"Yes, don't let anyone go into the coatroom. Did you see Hank Meeler go in there a few minutes ago? Or anyone else?"

Her face got even whiter and she started to shake. "No."

"Hey, I'm not blaming you for anything. I'm just asking some questions."

"I—I had to go to the bathroom. I figured it was a good time. No one seemed ready to leave. I—I wasn't gone long."

"It's okay. Your job wasn't to guard the place. You didn't do anything wrong. Calm down. Just stay right here and don't let anyone go in there."

"What's wrong?"

"Never mind. Don't go in there yourself." I took her arm and squeezed it. "Listen, I need you to get hold of yourself. This is very important. Can you do this for me?"

"Yes." She took a deep breath. "I'm okay now."

"Good." I left Paka taking photos and the girl standing guard. I hoped people wouldn't give her a bad time. I spoke to those gathered near me. "There's been an accident here." Yeah, not for one minute did I believe there had been an accident, that Hank Meeler had shot himself. "I'm taking charge until the police arrive. No one should leave the room." I looked around for someone I could trust.

"What's wrong, Jo?" Olen Judd spoke to me.

"Olen, we have a problem. Will you go to the front door and make sure no one leaves the building?"

Olen looked at me with a question on his face. I didn't volunteer any information about the problem. Announcing that Hank Meeler had been shot would cause a panic. I realized that the shooter could have already left. He or she could have slipped out the minute Corki started screaming.

Finally two uniformed policemen walked toward where I stood. I recognized one of them from my days working for the newspaper—Ernie Dodswell.

He remembered me too. "Jolene Allen, what are you up to now?"

I knew I had a reputation for being the first reporter on the scene at any event in Hot Springs and Garland County that made news. "We have a serious problem here, Dods. You'll want to call for backup. You need to secure the building."

"Still telling me how to do my job?" He grinned.

"Trust me on this one, Dods." I pointed to the coatroom.

He stepped inside and stepped back out, his face pale. He picked up the phone at the coatroom desk and called for help. Then he made an announcement.

"Okay, folks, no one leaves the room. Move away from here. Go back to the party."

Reactions were varied. Most people turned and walked away quietly, whispering to each other. A couple of women already wore jackets as if they meant to leave and hadn't.

We'd be here all night if the police decided to talk to each person at the party before they left. More than likely, they'd talk to some now, get a list, and talk to others later.

I turned to see Dods push Paka out of the coatroom. He would know she'd taken photos. If he said anything to her, I didn't hear it.

"I wish I hadn't poured that martini out," Paka said. She took deep breaths as if she hadn't breathed the whole time she was in the coatroom. "What's going on here, Jo?"

"I don't know, Paka, but I think I could use something stronger than a Coke myself. Let's get a big cup of black coffee. I think we're going to be at this party longer than we'd planned."

CHAPTER 3

About an hour had gone by when Paka hurried up to me. I was sitting at a table writing the story I planned to slip under the door of the newspaper office. "Jo, I need your help. Come talk to Ernie Dodswell."

"What's the matter, Paka?" The look on her face told me it was serious. I got up and walked beside her toward the coatroom.

"You aren't going to believe this. Dods thinks I shot Hank Meeler. He's going to take me in for questioning."

I stared at her. "No way. How could he even begin to think you killed Hank Meeler?"

"Someone set me up, Jo. One of the policemen found a gun in my camera bag. They think it's the murder weapon."

"You don't carry a gun." I stared at Paka.

"Of course I don't. You know that. I've got no reason to carry a gun—but I do have a permit." Paka kept walking fast. I practically had to run to keep up.

"Why do you have a permit?"

"It's a long story—and it has nothing to do with this."

So there were a few things about Paka I didn't know. I couldn't believe it. We told each other everything. "Didn't you have your bag with you all evening?" My mind raced to think of ways to prove what had happened was impossible.

"Sort of. I set it down all over the room in order to take photos. Anyone could have slipped the gun in it at any time."

"Not just any time. After they used it. You'd have found a gun in there earlier."

I could see Paka's mind racing too. "I had reloaded my camera just before Corki started screaming. I thought we were finished, but I never carry an empty camera. Then—" Paka traced her steps, trying to remember setting the bag down again. "I probably set it down before I went into the coatroom to take photos of Hank's body."

"You didn't take it in there with you?"

"I really can't remember. I don't think I did. I moved around that cramped space, took photos from all angles. I—I don't think I had the bag with me."

We caught up to Dods talking to the coat check girl. "Dods—" I grabbed his arm. He swung around.

"Don't argue with me, Jo. I know you and Paka are friends. That's why I let her come talk to you. You can go along, but I have to take her to the station for questioning. She had the gun in her bag, for God's sake. What do you want me to do? Ignore that?"

Ernie Dodswell was about to lose it. As competent as he was, I could probably count the murders he'd investigated on one hand—especially this kind of case. We didn't get a lot of murders in Hot Springs. Assault, robberies, mugging old people—plenty of that stuff from kids needing money for drugs or smokes. No murders at parties with well-dressed people. No killings of the city's wealthiest men.

"Okay, Dods, calm down. We'll come in and explain everything. I'll go with you, Paka. This won't take long."

It took the rest of the night. Paka argued. I argued. Someone ran a powder burn test on Paka's hands. The test was negative, but they said she could have washed her hands. She argued that powder burns don't wash off completely for days.

Finally I lost patience. "Ernie Dodswell, you know Paka didn't kill Hank Meeler. Someone put that gun in Paka's bag. That's obvious."

"Nothing is obvious here. And I don't know that Paka didn't kill Meeler. Neither do you." Dods paced back and forth, back and forth across his tiny office. He had drunk so much coffee, I knew his stomach had to be burning. That didn't make him any more pleasant.

"Why would she do such a thing? What motive could she possibly have?"

Paka got quiet. Too quiet. I stared at her. She looked scared, just plain scared.

"What?" I asked. "Did you have something going with Meeler? Why would you want to kill him?"

"I didn't want to kill him, Jo, but I was angry at him," Paka said. "In fact, I had a big fight with him just a couple of days ago. I might as well tell you and Ernie, since he'll find out."

Dods brightened up. "I knew it."

"You don't know anything, Dods," Paka said. "I would never kill anyone because I was angry with him."

"Tell your story, Paka." I was bone tired, but I sat down to listen.

Paka paced the floor. "Hank Meeler bought the mortgage on Mama's house. He bought up all the mortgages on the block. We didn't know this until last week. Meeler was calling in the loan. He insisted that Mama sell him her property. He'd pestered her to sell for a long time. Our whole block is zoned business."

"Why didn't you come to me, Paka, as soon as you found out? Your mother can't have much of a mortgage left. You've lived there forever."

"I didn't want to tell you, Jo. I wasn't going to take money from you, and neither was Mama. We were determined to keep it from you."

I felt even worse, if that was possible. I would have given Paka's mother anything she wanted. She should have known that.

"Lou, my kid brother—" Paka paused to tell Dods who Lou was. "He wanted to go to college. Mama wanted him to go. He got a partial scholarship at the university to play basketball. After one year, he'd get a full scholarship. Mama borrowed the money by refinancing her house to pay for his first year. She didn't ask me before she signed the papers. She didn't read the clause that said the bank was free to sell the mortgage. When I found out about Meeler buying it, I stomped into his office. I was as mad as hell, but I didn't kill him. What good would that do? I just told him I'd find the money by the time the loan was due."

"Paka—"

"Maybe I'd have come to you, Jo—as a last resort. But

my grandfather Bumpa and I had a plan."

I let out a long huff of air. I could see where Paka was coming from, but she had to know I'd help her if I could. Anytime.

"Wait a minute." I had a flash of memory that proved Paka didn't kill Meeler. "We heard the gunshot, Dods. Remember, Paka? You said someone was popping champagne corks from bottles. I said it sounded like a gunshot. It was a gunshot, and Paka was standing right beside me at the time."

"You're an unreliable witness, Jo," Dods told me. "How do I know you didn't just make that up?"

"I remember, Jo. You said I didn't have any experience with champagne," Paka said.

"Dods, you haven't formally charged Paka. Hold off. You can do that. I promise she won't leave town. She'll go home with me and I'll lock her in her darkroom. We need the photos she took tonight. You know if she killed Meeler, she wouldn't be stupid enough to put the gun back in her camera case."

Dods pulled his lips into a thin line and rubbed his chin. "People under stress do stupid things."

"Take my word for it, you're under a lot of stress, Dods." I stared at him. He looked away, fiddled with a pencil, tapped it on some papers for a few minutes.

"Okay, I'm not ready to arrest anyone here. But, Paka, I suggest you start looking for a good lawyer."

"Thanks, Dods." I grabbed Paka's arm and tugged her toward the door before Dods changed his mind. We could all use some sleep before one of us did something foolish.

CHAPTER 4

I rolled over, looked at the clock, groaned, and snapped awake. Pictures and voices from the night before flew through my head. I'd had only about four hours of sleep, but that would have to do for now. Setting my feet solid on the floor, I stood. The tantalizing smell of coffee, set up with a timer when we'd come in about 3 A.M., filled my nostrils.

I slipped a terry cloth muumuu over my head and padded to the kitchen on bare feet. Paka's pink sweater looked like a pool of Jell-O melting around her arms and hair on the breakfast table.

I poured two cups of black java and slid into the plastic seat of the booth opposite her. "Champagne hangover?" I asked, letting a grin spread over my face. I pushed her cup close enough to let the smell tempt her. "You didn't go to bed when we came in, did you?"

"Bed," she mumbled. "What's that?"

"It's what I pointed you toward early this morning."

She sat up, stretched, yawned, and pulled the mug close, cupping her hands around it as if she were cold. "I couldn't sleep. You don't think Dods really thinks I killed Hank Meeler, do you? I know the evidence looks bad, but I swear to you, Jo, I didn't. I wouldn't ruin my life, or yours, for that matter, doing such a thing. I have a bad temper. I'd be the first to admit it, but not that bad. Not crazy bad."

"I know that, Paka. We have to put the possibility of your being arrested out of our minds for now. Let's just concentrate on our work, what we do best. I have faith in Dods, in the police's ability to do their job." I had to say that to Paka, whether I believed it or not. I did believe it on one level, but I also thought Ernie Dodswell was in over his head with this kind of murder case.

"You have faith in the system, girl? And you still believe in Santa Claus and the Easter Bunny? I'll bet you'd still put a tooth under your pillow if someone knocked it out." Paka's sarcastic outlook on life was alive and well. I hoped she could hang on.

"You spent the last four hours in the darkroom?" I asked.

"Yeah."

Paka had a permanent reservation for the guest room at my place on the lake. Some of her clothes were in the closet. Extra drugstore junk was in the attached bath. I had suggested she set up her darkroom in a section of the boathouse when we were in high school. She had added to the space and improved her equipment, but it was still there. It made sense. We seldom worked alone. My stories and her photos went together for the package we turned out. She had done a few portraits for friends and family over the years. But I had never sold a story or article without her pictures.

I had begged her to move in with me after my parents

died. I took their old room, leaving my room vacant. But she said she needed a place of her own. She kept a small apartment in town. Unlike me, she had a boyfriend, a big family, a life besides work. And some secrets, it seemed, that I planned to worm out of her. A permit for a gun? Why?

Bumpa, Paka's grandfather, had moved into the apartment over the boathouse when my parents died. He had been caretaker for our place on the lake ever since I could remember. His wife had died about the same time my parents were killed. Out of mutual need, we agreed that he should live out here full time.

I was grateful. The place would have been too big, too lonely, without someone else around. I swallowed hard and let a wave of grief sweep over me and go on. I didn't have time for personal emotion right now. Scooting across the red plastic seat, I took my coffee out on the screened back porch. I stood, sipped the bitter liquid, and looked out over the lake.

A few geese and the ever present coots sailed along near the shore. A blue jay scolded from a hickory tree limb. *Scree, scree. Julio, julio, julio.* I loved the pesky birds, even though they terrorized the small birds that came to my feeders. I put out shelled corn just for them, but it was never enough. A cardinal floated down into my holly tree. Berries weren't red yet, but he looked like a red ribbon decorating the pointed leaves. *What cheer, what cheer, what cheer?*

"None," I said, and turned to go back into the living room. I put on my good mother voice. "Paka, you go get some sleep. Since I called and said it was coming, the *Sentinel* surely used the story we slipped under the door this morning. I assume they used file photos. I'll write a follow-up article using some of your new photos and get it to the newspaper by noon." I glanced at my watch. "Maybe."

"You just assuming this is our story?" Paka asked.

"Of course it is. The story was ours before Hank Meeler got shot. They wouldn't dare assign it to anyone else now." Even if you're involved, I said to myself.

Paka shrugged. I hurried out to the driveway to find the morning newspaper.

Shena and Sui bounced and danced, assuming we were going for their walk. Shena offered me her paw for a good-morning shake. Sui, her fuzzy white puppy who was bigger than his mom, took hold of my robe and tugged.

"Okay, okay, let me get dressed and we'll go for your walk. Be patient." Ha, as if they would.

I grabbed the rolled newspaper and started back to the door. Both dogs sat down and assumed their saddest faces.

"Guilt, oh yes, guys, I feel so guilty. But I'll be back." They didn't believe me, but I would. I needed a walk to clear my brain this morning.

I plopped the newspaper onto the kitchen table and smoothed out the folds. Hank Meeler's face stared up at me. And the bold headline read: LOCAL REALTOR MURDERED.

Who was it that said if you read it in the newspaper, it's true? I had seen Hank on the floor, seen the spilled blood, been there, done that. But this morning, I found it was hard to believe. Poor Corki. She didn't need this. She didn't deserve this.

I poured myself another cup of coffee, sat down, and re-read the article. Not bad, considering I wrote it at the country club and put the finishing touches on it at the police station. I knew the police had kept everyone except us at the party forever asking questions, getting details. No member of our graduating class was going to forget this reunion.

"Here they are." Paka returned, wearing jeans. Her T-shirt showed a cat looking in a mirror, a lion staring back. YOU ARE WHO YOU THINK YOU ARE. Paka the pussycat, really a lion. The shirt suited her. She is not a killer lion, though, not a murderer.

She plopped down a handful of 8 x 10 photos that slid across the table with a hiss. Black-and-white party faces smiled at me. Except for the last four. Hank Meeler's body.

"I guess by now Dods knows you have these?"

"Yes," Paka answered. "He said he wanted copies of every photo I took last night. Can they do that?"

"They can do anything they like. This is a murder investigation. And under the circumstances, I suggest you cooperate."

"Yeah, I guess you're right. Here's the lot. One package for them; one for the newspaper; these are ours."

"You giving the *Sentinel* photos of the body?" I asked.

"No. Doesn't seem right, or necessary. And the coroner's office will have sent over their photographer. I sure don't want to see this on the front page. Do you?"

"No, and I don't want Corki and her kids to have to see it either," I replied. "They have enough to deal with."

The phone rang. I looked at Paka. "Ed." She grinned, held out her hand for me to slap. I slapped and answered.

We were right. The caller was Ed the Editor. That really was his name. "Edward Zwink, rhymes with ink," he liked to say when he introduced himself. "What else could I have become?"

"I'm expecting another story, Jo, and Paka's photos by noon. Thanks for the story under the door. Harding followed the cop car last night, but this is all yours. He can do the behind-the-scenes work. You start doing your own interviews and see what the police will give you. Check out anyone who might have had a motive: business dealings, enemies, anything. I can get a credit report. Look at debts. Did Meeler gamble, bet the ponies? You look at the personal angle. Who was he sleeping with? Who had he ever slept with?"

"Ed, Hank has a family," I warned.

"We have a duty to find out who killed Hank Meeler. The truth is always in good taste."

"Maybe," I muttered and hung up. I had more than a duty. Finding out the truth about who killed Hank Meeler would be my number one priority for more reasons than a story. "Noon." I glanced at my watch and changed my mind. "No way. But this is my job right now, Paka. Get some sleep or you'll be no good to me at all."

"You win. I'm outta here." Paka stumbled off toward her room. She could sleep anytime, anyplace. She'd wake up full of ideas.

I stared at the photo of Hank and Corki, arms around each other, big smiles. The picture would stare up at me in tomorrow's paper. Was it my imagination or Paka's creative photo developing? I felt I could see dark shadows in the background behind them both.

What were you hiding, Hank, Corki? Did you really have a wonderful marriage, or was it a facade? Are there skeletons in the family or in the bedroom or in the closets of that million-dollar mansion you lived in on the lake? With Paka's sharp eyes and my curiosity—not to mention the need to keep Paka out of prison for a crime she didn't commit—I was going to find out.

CHAPTER
5

I tugged on a pair of jeans, soft with wear. The trouble with jeans is that about the time I get them broken in, they get holes. These had a tear across the knee and a frayed seat. I kept wearing them on my back roads and in the woods because I could wipe dog slobber on them.

Outside, I sat on the park bench under a pine tree and tied my shoes. Shena and Sui forgave the delay. They danced and spun and then Shena took the lead down the dirt road toward the corner. Sui trotted alongside me, looking up and smiling.

"Yes, we're walking, and you're a good dog." That was what he was waiting for. He took off into the woods after a rustle that might mean a rabbit or a deer. The woods around me belonged to a lot of small animals, snakes, toads, and birds. I loved my birds. For a few minutes, I let my mind go free and listened for their songs.

The morning was quiet. The only sound besides birdsongs was the crunch of my feet on gravel. My mom had loved walking every morning. The woods would always remind me of her, how she loved them. I took a deep breath and wished the dogs would come back, make some noise.

Neither dog was a barker. The last time I remember hearing Shena's voice was to warn me of a rattlesnake around the corner of the path into the woods. I had slowed, called her to me, and let the snake slither away. I might kill a poisonous snake in the yard, but I wouldn't kill one in the woods. My snake policy was: You stay out of my space, I'll respect yours.

Snakes. Snake in the grass. Skeleton in the closet. Murderer at the reunion. My mind made the connection to the subject I needed to think about. I pushed emotions, things I couldn't think about now, to the back of my mind.

I had seldom written a story for the newspaper about Hot Springs criminals. I didn't respect them. I found them boring and refused to give them any publicity. Drugs, small robberies, domestic violence—that was the makeup of crime in our city.

The murder of a well-known man put me in a different mindset. A man I knew. A man who seemed to have everything. I read a lot, mostly mysteries, but I also enjoy true crime stories. I find the mind of an intelligent criminal fascinating. What makes a person choose to live on the dark side? What hurts and disappointments will fester inside a person? What anger boils until that person is able to kill?

That was how I'd approach this story. I would paint the background of Hank Meeler's life, but I'd also start to paint a picture of his killer.

"Come on, doggies," I called. I jogged off on a path that led back to the house. I was eager to get to work.

*   *   *

I was chewing a raisin-cinnamon bagel covered with cream cheese and looking at Paka's photos when the phone rang. I kept my finger on the picture of a man talking to Hank Meeler. What was J.D. Stroud doing at the reunion? He wasn't in our high school class. Not by a long shot. He was at least ten years older and ten years richer. Stroud was a well-known Hot Springs bookie. In and out of trouble, most of the time he operated on the edge of the law. He was the kind of lawyer that kept lawyer jokes going, but his law background kept him out of jail.

"Jolene Allen here. Good morning."

"Jo, did I wake you? I'm so glad you're home."

I thought for a moment. "Corki? Is that you?" Her voice was hoarse as if she'd been up all night crying.

"Jo," she answered, "I need help. I don't know who else to turn to. Who else I can trust. And I have to talk to someone."

"Corki, you don't want to talk to me," I told her. "I'm writing this story for the newspaper." I had wondered how I was going to get Corki to talk to me. But I didn't want her to share personal things, information I couldn't use.

"I know you better than you think, Jo. I know you stayed calm and took charge last night. I know you have a lot of integrity. I believe you can let me talk off the record and not use what I say in a story."

"Why don't you talk to Anilee?" I asked. "She was Hank's partner."

"I don't know Anilee that well. I've stayed out of Hank's business on purpose. Also—she could be involved in some of this."

"Is there a relative you could talk to?" I asked.

"I don't have any close relatives here, well, none that I trust," Corki answered.

"Some other friend?"

"I—I'm sure you will find this strange, Jo, but I don't have any close friends."

No friends? Corki Meeler? This was the biggest piece of news I'd heard since high school. She had fooled me. She seemed like the most popular woman in town. What could I say? I thought of how badly I had needed friends when my mother and father were killed. How Paka and Bumpa and their whole family had been there for me. I swallowed the bite of bagel that was stuck in my throat. "Of course I'll help you, Corki," I told her. "What can I do?"

"I—I feel awkward talking about finances at a time like this. But—I've been up all night. I thought we were rich, Jo, as rich as we needed to be. This morning, I called about funeral arrangements, and I can't get credit at the funeral home. I called our lawyer, and I've found out I may lose everything. We are on the verge of bankruptcy."

She paused and sniffed, her voice full of tears. Then she continued, "That's not all. Sometimes Hank hid cash in the house. For emergencies, he said. I started looking for money. Instead, I found a note in Hank's underwear drawer, hidden away."

"What kind of note, Corki?" I thought of several types. A love letter. A threatening note. A loan receipt. "Whatever it is, shouldn't you give it to the police?" I questioned.

"I don't want to, Jo. I'm afraid—"

"Does it threaten you?"

"No." She was quiet for so long I thought she had hung up. Changed her mind about sharing secrets with me. But

I'd heard no click, and I wasn't getting a dial tone. I took a deep breath and waited.

"Oh, Jo," Corki whispered, "I'm afraid Hank was keeping all sorts of secrets from me. I guess I'll have to give this to the police. Before then, can you come over? Please. I don't want to tell you any more on the phone." Corki started to sob.

"Hang on, Corki. I'll be there in a half hour."

I took the world's fastest shower. Then I grabbed a better pair of jeans, a T-shirt, purse, my notebook, and tape recorder. I tucked the photos I'd chosen for the article I was writing—sometime—into an envelope and stuck those in my briefcase. I wished Paka could go with me, but she needed some sleep. Also Corki might not talk to us both. I might not be able to write what Corki told me, but I had a feeling she was going to blow this story wide open.

CHAPTER
6

I live on a cove of Lake Hamilton. My road leads only to my house. Corki and Hank Meeler live in a huge house on the same lake, but I had to drive back out to the highway and down another road to get there. Their property was secured by a high iron fence and a gate set into a rock wall. I stopped my car, got out, and used the intercom phone set into a box in the wall to identify myself. By the time I got back into my car, the gate swung open.

The house was old, but the Meelers had remodeled and added on when they bought it. I didn't know why anyone wanted or needed such a big house, but, hey, it was their money. And they had a beautiful view of the lake and surrounding mountains.

A maid let me in and showed me to the room where Corki was. She sat at a big desk, shuffling papers around. "Jo, oh, Jo, this is such a mess. I never would have looked at it this morning, but I needed to do something. And then when I called the funeral home and our lawyer, well—" Corki closed her eyes and took a deep breath.

She looked as if she had cried all night. Her hair was limp and hung around her face. Her skin, without makeup, was red and blotchy. Her thin lips were pulled into a grim line. She looked so plain, not the glamorous woman I had always seen in public. Not the beauty who often stared at me from the society page of the newspaper.

The maid returned with coffee and a plate of cinnamon rolls. I wasn't hungry, but once I smelled the cinnamon, I reached for one and tore off a bite. Eating would give me something to do while I waited for Corki to talk. She had laid her head on her arms on the messy desk.

Finally I broke the silence. "Corki, should I come back later? When did you eat last? Maybe a cup of coffee would help."

"No, no, don't leave. I need to talk to someone. You're right." She sat up, ran her fingers through her hair, and poured coffee into a thin china cup. A dollop of cream turned the coffee a caramel color. I sipped from my own cup and waited.

She took one bite of a roll, finished her drink, set the cup down with a clink. She wiped her mouth and took another deep breath. "I found this in Hank's dresser." She handed me a piece of paper. The note had been wadded up, smoothed back out, folded once.

I took the paper and stared. Words had been cut from a magazine and pasted to read:

YOU RUINED MY LIFE. SAYING SORRY IS NO HELP. I HAVE DECIDED TO TAKE YOURS. YOU CAN WORRY ABOUT WHEN I WILL DO THIS. WATCH YOUR BACK!

"When did Hank get this?"

"I have no idea. I never saw it until today."

"So he could have gotten this letter a year ago or last week?"

Corki nodded and sniffed. She searched the pockets of her bathrobe for a tissue.

"Do you have any ideas about who might have sent it?" I asked.

"No. I think it's the kind of thing a woman would do, not a man, don't you?"

I sort of agreed. But I had been in the newspaper business long enough to know an angry or disturbed man or woman will do strange things. Behavior, male or female, is hard to predict.

"Corki, money wasn't the only reason you went through Hank's dresser drawers, was it?" I might as well dig as deep as possible while Corki was willing to talk.

"Jo, I know you're writing a story for the paper. But this is just between you and me. Okay?" She reached out and touched my arm, pleading.

"Sure, Corki." I hoped I could keep my promise.

"I've suspected for some time that Hank was seeing another woman."

"Just one?" I had to ask.

"Well, I think so. But he had changed in the last couple of years. We pretended in public, but we weren't as close as we once had been. Hank was quiet all the time, hard to talk to. Distant, even cold. At first I thought he was worried about something. A real estate deal. Business in general. I don't know. I never asked him about business or money. I guess that seems funny to you, but I didn't care. And I'm not very smart. I had my interests, my charities. Last week, though, I asked him if we could take a vacation together. I thought if he got away from here— Well, maybe we could talk, have a good time. Laugh and play like we used to do. I missed the old Hank."

I picked up on one thing she said. "You're a lot smarter than you think, Corki. Sometimes a man likes to make a woman think she's dumb. He just wants her on his arm, looking pretty."

She looked at me. "And I did that, didn't I? I played the good little wife."

I never thought I'd feel sorry for Corki Meeler. I reached out, took her hand, and squeezed it. "You have to be strong now," I told her. "You have to give this note to the police. And you have to find out what was bothering Hank. If it was business, Anilee Mowdy should know. Or his lawyer."

"After I called our lawyer this morning, he called me back. Hank was deep in debt. There's no money. He warned me that creditors would start to call immediately."

"Your number is unpublished, isn't it?" I asked. "Let your maid answer the phone."

Corki nodded. "Larry—my lawyer—said he'd sit down with me and show me what he knows."

I needed to talk to some other people. I would help Corki, but Corki could help me too.

"Get dressed, Corki. When someone close dies, you should get to hide and mourn in private. But I think knowing what's going on with *your* life may be more important."

"What do you want me to do?" she asked.

"You can talk to the lawyer again later. Let's go find out what Anilee Mowdy knows," I said.

CHAPTER 7

I made some phone calls while Corki cleaned up. She came back looking like the woman I knew from her photos and last night's party.

I had called Anilee Mowdy to warn her that we were coming. She was in her office and said she planned to stay there.

"Where are the kids, Corki?" I asked as we got into my car.

"I sent them to Hank's sister's place for several days. I know they need me, and I'll be there for them, but I needed some time to—to—" She looked out the car window.

"I know, Corki. You don't need to apologize for anything you do for yourself. I know Hank's sister Beth from her work with foster children. She's wonderful with kids."

"I didn't know you knew her," Corki said. "When I called you—well, I couldn't tell Beth about Hank—that Hank might be—"

"You can't protect her," I warned. "Or the kids. This is all going to come out eventually."

"I know." Corki said nothing more while I drove us to town. I left her to whatever was tumbling through her head. I mentally made a list of people I wanted to talk to after we saw Anilee.

The first thought I had when we walked into Meeler & Mowdy—Meeting Your Real Estate Needs for the Future— was how attractive Anilee was except for the dark circles under her eyes. Could she be the woman that Hank Meeler was involved with? No, I decided almost immediately. Anilee was too smart to mix business with pleasure.

She wore a dark red suit, sparkling white blouse with a tied bow in front, perfectly matching shoes, and silver jewelry. Her black hair was blunt cut to swing free and frame her face just at her chin. Neat, stylish, efficient. I summed up my impression of Hank's partner.

"Corki, how are you this morning?" She hugged Corki and blew an air kiss past her ear. "Surely we're living in the same bad dream."

Corki nodded but said nothing. I suspected she didn't trust her voice, and her eyes were filled with tears. She was strong, though, strong enough to be out here with me the day after her husband was killed.

Enough of the polite talk. "Anilee," I began, "Corki has found out that Hank has money problems. What do you know about that?"

Anilee pointed to two chairs. She sighed and settled in another chair behind her huge desk. "Not as much as I should have known. I knew we'd had a rocky year. I didn't know Hank's private financial dealings."

"Will his private bank accounts, or lack of, affect the financial state of your business?" I hoped she'd be honest with us.

"Of course." Anilee played with a pearl-colored pen on her desk. She took a deep breath and said, "This is going to come out in the investigation, Corki, so I might as well be the one to tell you."

Corki seemed to come out of her moment of self-pity to pay attention to Anilee. "Sounds like more bad news." She almost smiled, even though this session was anything but funny.

"I have always respected Hank's office, his desk, but under the circumstances, I felt it was okay to snoop around. Corki, I just discovered that Hank was keeping two sets of books on the business."

"You don't have an accountant?" I asked.

"No, Hank has always done the bookkeeping. We have a tax man and a lawyer, of course. But Hank said he was a business and math major, and why pay someone else to add and subtract? I could look at the record books any time I wished," Anilee explained.

"But you didn't know there were two sets of books," I said. "How long had this been going on?"

"The whole time we've been in business." Anilee threw her pen at a stack of papers. Her lips pulled into a grim line. A scowl spread across her face.

"I'm sorry, Anilee." Corki bit her lip and tried to keep from falling apart.

"Hank's actions are not your fault, Corki." Anilee's voice was firm, businesslike. "If I didn't know what he was doing at work, how could you?"

She emphasized "at work." I took that to mean that she knew about Hank's life after work. We were here to get information. I jumped into the mud with both feet. "Anilee, Corki suspects that Hank was having an affair. Do you know anything about that?"

"How long have you known?" Anilee asked Corki.

"I didn't *know*, Anilee," Corki answered. "I suspected. Don't worry about my feelings. I—I might as well know everything. The police will find out. I'd rather hear it from you."

Anilee uncapped her pen and doodled on the back of an envelope for a few seconds. I felt like I was stuck in the middle of a soap opera where all I could do was listen and watch. "He was careful," Anilee said, "but I'm sure he's been seeing Venice Harwood."

"Venice?" I don't know why I was surprised.

You ruined my life. I remembered the diamond earrings that Venice wore so proudly. That she flaunted, I'd say, now that I knew the truth. Could it ruin Venice's life to get involved with Hank Meeler? She didn't look or act depressed or angry last night, but she was an actress. She might have been "on stage" all evening.

Corki seemed to put Hank's personal life aside. "How bad are the finances here, Anilee? Hank had that big business deal last year. The one where you sold all the land to the new luxury hotel and spa."

"The one where we sold the land Hank bought for so little from Ray Chronister?" Anilee asked.

Corki hesitated. "Yes, he said he was gambling to buy all that property when he did, and that the gamble paid off."

"I left all the industrial and business properties to Hank," Anilee said. "My speciality is homes, private estates." Fingers fiddled with the pen again. "But I think Hank knew how valuable Ray's property was going to be before when he bought it. I think he already had a deal in the works."

"Are you saying he cheated Ray?" Corki asked. "Hank and Ray have been friends since childhood."

"When are you cheating someone and when are you making a good business deal?" Anilee shrugged. "I know Ray was really angry when he found out how much Hank resold the property for."

"Angry enough to kill Hank?" I asked. Anilee might as well know I was investigating the murder for the newspaper. And for Paka, I reminded myself. Paka might have motive, but I was glad to find out she wasn't the only one who held a grudge against Hank Meeler.

"Are you writing all I'm saying into a piece for the newspaper, Jo? Don't you dare quote me." Anilee squared her shoulders, ready for a fight.

"Right now, I'm just fishing, Anilee. I am writing an article about the murder for the *Sentinel Record*, but I deal in facts, not your opinions. I'll talk to Ray myself. I'll ask him how angry he was," I replied.

"Jo," Corki said, "you need to be careful. I've heard that when someone kills once, they don't hesitate to kill again."

"You live out there on the lake by yourself, Jo," Anilee said. "Doesn't that make you nervous?"

"Why should it? I've lived there all my life. And I'm not really alone. Paka's grandfather, Jake Powell, has been living in the apartment over my boathouse since his wife died."

"Maybe you should consider selling, Jo," Anilee said. "The place must hold sad memories for you. And that lakefront property is worth a fortune. I could show you some great condos in town or in Hot Springs Village."

"When did this discussion go from being about Hank to being about me?" I felt put out at Anilee. I'd never sell. I'd never move off the lake. I loved it there. I had great memories, and I didn't want to move away from them.

"Sorry, Jo, we did get off the subject, but keep what I've said in mind. You may have enemies you don't even know about from your days at the newspaper. And when it gets out that you're asking questions, writing articles about Hank's murder— Well, watch your back." Anilee took the batch of papers in front of her and stacked them in neat piles. "Did you know that Hank liked to bet the ponies, Corki?"

"He loved to go to the races at Oaklawn. We went together to opening day. A lot of people in Hot Springs like horse racing," Corki explained. However, she didn't answer Anilee's question.

"Did you know he had lost a lot of money on the horses, Corki, and that he didn't just bet during the season in Hot Springs?"

Corki sighed and looked at her fingernails. The bright red polish was chipped badly. Had she worried them all last evening and today? "No," she said. "I guess he thought if he won big, he could get back on his feet."

I remembered the photo of J.D. Stroud at the party. Did Hank owe him money? Stroud was not a man who would grant me a polite interview. I'd put the police onto Meeler's gambling habits. They probably knew by now. Dods was smart and efficient. I hoped he wanted some other suspects except Paka, that he wouldn't think he had the murderer and relax.

"Anilee," Corki asked, "do you think my house—our house—? We had it paid for. Do you think Hank—?"

"An expensive property is one of the easiest sources of money. I'll see what the bank says. Look, Corki, I know you've never liked me very much, but we need to work together on this."

"I don't dislike you, Anilee," Corki said, sitting up straighter. "On the contrary, I admire you a lot. I wish I had a head for business. I've just always stayed out of Hank's business life. I guess that was a mistake."

I saw an opportunity here. "Anilee, I have an idea. Why don't you do some calling right now? I don't think you want to be seen in public, but you and Corki can order in some lunch while you outline a plan. Then you take Corki home. I've got a lot of leads to follow up, and I want to get started now. Okay with you, Corki?"

"I—I guess so. I don't really want to be in that big house alone," Corki said. I could understand that. "And thanks, Jo. Can I call you again?"

"Please do. I'll be upset with you if you don't. Call me day or night. Remember, I'm alone too."

We stood up and she hugged me. I felt guilty thinking of Corki as a story before I thought of her personal needs. I would be there for her. It wouldn't hurt me to make some new friends. Paka and I had been a pair, a partnership for so long, I'd never looked farther for a social life. But now I remembered that Corki had called when my parents were killed. She had stopped and brought food herself. I had written her a formal thank-you note, but I hadn't appreciated her concern.

I hugged her back. Then I reached out and shook hands with Anilee Mowdy. I left before I started crying. Nothing like new wounds, new hurts, to open up old ones—old ones that had just barely started to heal.

I stopped in the hall, dropped some quarters into the drink machine, waited till a Coke rolled out. I grasped the cold can and held it to my cheeks on the way to my car. Then I popped the top, took a long drink, and swallowed both the soda and the lump in my throat. Next I flipped through the phone book I kept in my car and punched in the number on my car phone for Venice and Eddie Harwood. I'd have liked to surprise her, but I'd give her fifteen minutes to paint her face and put on her diamond earrings.

CHAPTER 8

As soon as I turned off the phone, I headed for Venice's house. I didn't want her to have time to leave, but southern women have to put on their makeup. I laughed to think about Venice scrambling to do so.

Sure enough, when she opened the door, she looked as if she was about to make her entrance on stage in a romantic comedy. She was wearing a red top and black tights that showed off her tiny figure. I noticed her red heart earrings right away. No diamonds. But all the makeup didn't hide red eyes and some wrinkles I hadn't seen last night. Was she crying because she'd had to kill Hank, or because someone else robbed her of his company?

"Venice, hi. Thanks for seeing me." Not that I'd given her a chance to say no. I stepped toward her, making her move back and let me into her living room. Her house was a small wood frame, close to the racetrack, not in the best part of town. I was sure it wasn't what Venice had in mind when she graduated from high school and hurried off to seek her fortune.

She hadn't had time to clean house or to get Eddie moved to another room. He slumped on the couch, only half dressed, newspaper spilled around him. The TV was blaring, tuned to some golf tournament. An ashtray spilled over with cigarette butts. A coffee cup and half-eaten piece of toast sat beside the ashtray. He looked at me but didn't speak.

I did. "Hi, Eddie. Guess it's hard to wait for racing season to start."

He didn't answer. Didn't jockeys work someplace else in off-season, riding and training horses? Maybe today was his day off. I realized it was Saturday. Last night seemed days ago.

"I was just fixing to make a fresh pot of coffee, Jolene," Venice said in a soft drawl. "Come on in the kitchen and talk to me. I'm feeling so sad this morning."

I could certainly see why she didn't want to talk in front of Eddie. If Eddie didn't know about Hank, she wanted to keep it secret. If she could. Another thought hit me. If Eddie did know, would he be angry enough to kill Hank? I added another suspect to my list.

I sat at the kitchen table, yellow Formica, surely left over from her mother's kitchen in the Fifties. The table was clean. An African violet bloomed in the center on a plastic mat.

"I'm sorry about Hank, Venice. I know you cared for him." I'd act as if everyone knew her relationship with Hank and see what she said.

"Why— Well, of course I liked Hank. Everyone did. He was the most popular boy in the senior class. I haven't seen much of him since I got back. Since I got married—but—"

"Oh, maybe my information is wrong." I played with my pen, doodling on a blank notebook page.

"What information?" She glanced toward the living room.

I kept my voice low. "Anilee Mowdy told me you were dating Hank." Dating. I almost laughed at my choice of words. Like in high school—sure she was dating.

"I don't know why she'd tell you a thing like that." Venice kept measuring coffee into the top of a Mr. Coffee machine. This was going to be a super strong brew. "We went to lunch a couple of times. I was looking at some houses. If Eddie wins big this spring, he promised me a new house. This one is so small. It was my mama's, you know."

I didn't know. Both of us were living in our parents' homes. "No, I didn't," I told her.

"It made sense for us to live here until Eddie gets the right horse. He's had really bad luck. You know, a horse can have terrific potential. Then he'll come up lame, or—or something."

In other words, Eddie always had an excuse for why he didn't win. "Are you working someplace, Venice? You don't have any children, do you?"

"No, not yet. We keep hoping. Until then, or until Eddie's horse comes in, I'm working at the racetrack. I work the gate or selling tickets in season. Off-season, there's always work to do. It's not the work I thought I'd be doing, Jo, but—" She shrugged. "Well, most people don't get to do what they planned, do they?"

"No, not many." I took the cup of coffee Venice handed me as soon as it finished dripping. The color was as black as shoe polish and smelled bitter like chicory. I added a lot of cream so I could drink it. "No, thanks," I said to the plate of donuts she offered me. If she ate many of them herself, she wouldn't stay under a hundred pounds. Unless the stress of being married to Eddie kept the pounds worried off. I could see why she'd be tempted by Hank's advances.

"You did, Jo," Venice said. "You and Paka followed your dream. Maybe if I hadn't gotten married as soon as I got back to Hot Springs— Well, I did. Mama wanted to see me married." She sat in front of her own coffee and twisted the side of her hair into a curl around her cheek.

"I'm writing a story for the newspaper, Venice. I'm talking to everyone who was still friends with Hank."

"You think one of his friends killed him?"

"I guess they'd have to be a former friend." I smiled.

"Jo, I didn't kill Hank. You know that, don't you? Why would I want to kill him?" She looked at me without blinking. I heard the sadness in her voice, saw the sorrow in her whole body. I couldn't forget, though, how good an actress she was at one time.

I wanted to believe her. "I never said you did, Venice. I'm just talking to people. Do you have any idea who might have wanted him dead? Did he ever say anything about someone who was mad at him? Someone who was bothering him, threatening him?"

"My goodness, no. Why would he talk to me about his enemies? I wouldn't have thought he'd have an enemy in the whole world. Everybody loved Hank."

"Not everyone." I took the last sip of my coffee. I'd be wired for two days. "Thanks for talking, Venice, and for the coffee. Why don't you get involved with the little theater here in town? I hear they're very good."

She kept sitting at the table, even when I got up. She stared at her own coffee, untouched. "That's a good idea. Maybe I will."

"I'll see myself out." I left her sitting there, lost in her own thoughts. I wanted to think she didn't kill Hank, but I could think of a dozen reasons why she would. He made promises he couldn't keep. He refused to leave Corki and go off with her. Maybe he was getting tired of her and wanted to break off their relationship and she didn't want to. Or back to my earlier thought: maybe Eddie found out, fought with Venice, and killed Hank. Venice might know or suspect that Eddie killed Hank. Maybe Eddie had even threatened her. She might be caught in a dark web she had woven for herself.

I took a deep breath of the warm fall air when I got outside. I had picked up on the heavy load of sorrow in the Harwood house and shook my head to get rid of it. My own load of unresolved grief was enough to handle. I couldn't help her, and I didn't need to share in Venice's broken dreams.

CHAPTER 9

I was hungry, but I headed for the newspaper office. I was able to borrow a computer and pound out my story, leaving out my meeting with Corki. The story was a rehash of the murder, who was at the reunion party, what was being done. I guessed at what the police were doing and added that no one had been arrested for the murder. Thank God that Dods decided not to book Paka, for now.

I handed Ed my photos and drove home. A time-out was what I needed. I'd wake Paka, and we'd look at her photos again, carefully. I had a feeling I'd discover more clues in them. People can lie. Photos can't—usually.

I pulled into my driveway, stepped out of the car, and immediately heard the dogs barking down in the woods. A chill ran the length of my spine. I wanted to think it was from stepping from the air-conditioned car into the sweaty heat of midday. I knew it wasn't.

"Okay, guys, I'll come check it out." I grabbed my snake stick, a hoe actually, from the corner of the garage and took a trail the deer and I had stomped in the underbrush. I wouldn't kill the snake unless I had to, but I wanted to be armed.

I stepped around poison ivy and kept going deeper into the tangle of oaks, hickories, blackberry bushes, and azaleas gone wild. Now the dogs were quiet, too quiet. The woods were silent. I stopped to listen. Nothing. No birdsongs, no rustles or sticks breaking from doggie feet. I stopped myself from calling out. First I wanted to see what had bothered them.

Rounding a huge oak, I nearly smacked into Ray Chronister. I raised the hoe before I could think or take in a familiar face.

"Hey, don't hit me, Jolene." He was half bent over, petting Shena, who was wagging her whole body, glad for the attention.

"What are you doing here, Ray?" My voice held anger, but I knew it covered my fear. I didn't want him to know I was afraid.

"Relax, Jo. Relax." He was extra jolly, and his voice slightly slurred, but surely he wasn't drunk at noon. "I was wondering if you'd consider selling this place to me. I've come into some money, and I've always wanted to live on the lake. I knocked on your door, but you weren't home. I went for a walk, and then the dogs found me. Nice dogs." He rubbed Sui's head. He had wiggled in front of Shena, jealous of her.

And why did they bark at you? I thought. They usually don't bark at people. I didn't have an answer to my question, so I addressed his. "I have no intention of selling my home, Ray. You could have asked me last night and saved yourself a trip." I wanted to ask him when he'd come into some money—where and how that had happened. But I didn't figure it was any of my business.

"I like coming out here. I've always liked this cove. It's so private. You sure you aren't lonely out here?" he asked.

"No, Ray, I'm not. Since you're here, I have a question for you." I started back to the house, suggesting to Ray that he leave. "I heard that Hank Meeler cheated you out of a lot of money."

Ray didn't answer immediately, just walked along behind me. I found I didn't want to turn my back on him, so I walked in a sideways shuffle. "That's one way to put it." His face had gotten redder. "He had been wanting my property on Highway Seven for a long time. I finally decided to sell it to him. My timing was bad."

"You think he had another deal in the works, even while he was buying yours? That he had the hotel people interested?"

"I'm sure he knew they were in town looking around."

"He could have called you and brokered the sale, collecting his eight or so percent, couldn't he?" I asked.

"A real friend would have done that. Yes," Ray replied.

"But you had been friends since you were kids." Shena licked my hand. I was glad to know she was right beside me.

"I thought we were friends. Maybe Hank thought of me as someone who hung around him all the time. I'm not sure anyone was really Hank's friend. I mean, in his thinking."

"You're saying your friendship wasn't two-way?" I asked. Maybe we were getting somewhere.

"Hank always had to win. At sports, then at business deals. He didn't care who he stepped on to be number one."

"Are you saying he had a lot of enemies?"

"I'd guess he did. I didn't hate him, Jo. He was a difficult person to hate. I didn't kill him, if that's what you're asking."

That *was* what I wanted to ask Ray. But, on the other hand, no one was going to confess because I asked the question.

"My guess is that Corki is the only one who's really crushed by his death. Maybe his kids. I don't know them," Ray explained.

We came into the yard on that note. I didn't want to make an enemy of Ray Chronister. "Tell you what, Ray. If I do decide to sell my place, I'll call you first. Give you first refusal."

"Thanks, Jo. And my other offer stands. If you're ever lonely, call me. I'll come over or take you to dinner. We could even go fishing together. I've always admired you."

"Thanks, Ray," I said and hurried into the house. Sorry, but I've never admired you. If I get lonely enough to call, I'll take two aspirin and reconsider in the morning.

"What's that little half smile doing on your lips, girl?" Paka stood in the kitchen window, watching Ray leave. "You falling for Ray Chronister after all these years?"

Her voice said, are you that desperate? I laughed. "Not likely. I was just thinking what I'd do if I did."

"Drown yourself." She yawned, stretched, and reached for her coffee cup. "Become bass bait." She giggled at the idea.

"I found him snooping in the woods," I explained to Paka. "He said he wanted to buy my place. He has come into money. Do you think he carried an insurance policy on Hank Meeler?"

"Stranger things have happened. Let's go check on Bumpa." Paka took her coffee onto the screened porch that looked out on the lake. I grabbed an apple, took a big bite, and followed her. Bumpa was a very sensible man. He might be a big help to us.

Paka said her grandfather used to ride the kids on his foot, up and down, up and down, saying, "Bumpa, bumpa, bumpa." They'd ask for the ride saying, "Bumpa." Then finally, that's what they called him.

Bumpa's real name was Jake. He cut the lawn, trimmed the trees, and kept the outbuildings from falling down. He and my dad had serviced our boats together. But it was Jake who kept everything shipshape. One of the reasons I felt safe on the lake was having Jake nearby.

We walked past Jake's big garden, abundant with squash, cantaloupe, and melons, not to mention huge, juicy tomatoes. He shared veggies and fruit with me since I had never been able to make anything but a few houseplants grow. And those thrived on neglect.

The boathouse had a concrete ramp that slid down to the lake's edge. This time of year, though, my party boat and speedboat were in the water, tied up to the dock. Only the canoe was stored when not in use. We climbed the outside stairs to Bumpa's back door.

"Hey, Bumpa, you in there?" Paka knocked, then went in.

"Who was that in the Buick, Jo?" Bumpa came from the front of his place to meet us. "I saw you come out of the woods with that man. I never saw his car drive up."

If I ever had a boyfriend, he'd have to pass Bumpa's inspection. "He parked in the pull-off," I said. Then I told Bumpa who my visitor was.

"You're not thinking of selling this place, are you, Jo?" Bumpa filled and set the teakettle on the stove.

"Of course not. I don't know how that rumor got started. And if I did, I'd sure talk it over with you first."

"If you ever get a boyfriend, make sure Bumpa knows

what kind of car he drives too," Paka said as she grinned at me. She had read my mind.

"I'm paid to know who's here," Bumpa said. "Want a cup of tea?" He was asking me. He knew Paka didn't. Tea cold, coffee hot was her rule.

I took another big bite of my juicy apple. "Sure, Bumpa." I looked at the picture on the puzzle box on the kitchen table. Bumpa always had a puzzle going, summer or winter. He said it helped him think. Paka collapsed in Bumpa's chair and stared at his puzzle.

"I'm getting McClard's barbeque for supper. You two join me?" Bumpa asked, pouring hot water into two cups. "Or do you have more parties to attend?"

"Parties have been canceled, Bumpa. You heard about Hank Meeler, didn't you?" I asked.

"I read the newspaper. Mr. Meeler liked his ponies. Maybe one just up and bit him." Bumpa scratched his head while he pulled out his paper and spread it open on top of his puzzle.

Bumpa liked his ponies too, but I knew he was a very conservative gambler. "You see Hank Meeler at the track a lot?"

"Every time I went there." Bumpa grinned. He usually got there every day during the season. Often only to watch or to bet two dollars. He'd brag when he won twenty, and that went into his fund to play again. It was a game for Bumpa. Sounded like it was an obsession for Hank. Or a desperate attempt to get quick money.

We sat at the table. I realized that Paka hadn't been in our conversation. She looked up at her grandfather, tears in her eyes. "Bumpa, somebody put the gun that shot Hank Meeler in my camera case. Now the cops think I shot him."

"Was it your gun?" Bumpa asked, stirring sugar into his tea, staring at the amber liquid.

"No. But they're going to dig deeper into this. Why I had a permit to carry."

Bumpa looked at Paka. There were tears in his eyes. "Paka, baby, I think you'd better tell Jolene everything."

"Everything? What? Tell me what?" I asked. A mouthful of tea scalded all the way down my throat.

"Jo, you have to understand, you're like a sister to me. I love you as much as anyone in my family. But some things are private. Some things need to stay in the family."

I looked at Paka and at Bumpa. Neither would look at me. "What things?"

"Years ago—I don't know—eight, I guess. I—I—" Paka looked at Bumpa, giving him permission to tell her story.

"That bastard Hank Meeler raped Paka, Jo," Bumpa explained. "Bessie was cleaning houses then. She cleaned the Meelers' house once a week. She got sick and was afraid she'd lose her job, so that day she sent Paka over to clean." Bumpa put out his hand to stop me from speaking. He wanted to finish. "You was up to Little Rock with your folks. Paka didn't have anything to do that day, so she went over there. She was there a couple of times before with Bessie to help out."

Paka was able to continue. "I fought him. He was so big and strong, but he said Mama would lose her job if I didn't—if I didn't let him—I didn't know what else to do."

"Didn't you tell someone? Go to the police?" I couldn't believe what I was hearing.

Paka looked at Bumpa and sighed. "You don't understand anything, Jo. Who was going to believe me when Hank denied my story?"

"So—so you didn't do anything? Go to the hospital? Tell anyone?"

"There are some things it's better to keep in a family, Jolene," Bumpa reasoned. "Me and Bessie and Paka talked it over. We agreed to keep it secret. Bessie quit her job, of course, and she got plenty of others. Neither she nor Paka realized how easily white folk would hire black folks to do their dirty work."

"Wait a minute, Bumpa. You and Paka are talking like some kind of Forties movie here. White folk. Black folk. Keeping things secret. You're—you're—"

"We're black, Jo," Paka said. "Maybe you forget that sometimes, but we don't. You may think you know everything about me, about my family, but you could never in a million years know what it's like to be black without stepping into my skin and living there for awhile."

I had nothing to say to that. I knew Paka was right. "So you *did* kill Hank Meeler?"

"If I was going to kill Meeler, Jo, I'd have done it eight years ago. If I had it to do over again, maybe I'd go to the police, write out an assault charge, and take my chances that someone would believe me. They got tests today, they could find out the truth. But what I did was I got scared. I was scared to go out of the house alone at night. Scared to go most anywhere except to work or out here, someplace with you. Bumpa helped me get a gun and a permit to carry it. I don't know why that helped, but it did. Or I thought it did. Same thing."

"God, I'm sorry, Paka. I didn't know. I didn't know." I jumped up, spilling my tea, and ran out of the house. I ran till I reached the dock, the lake, and couldn't run any farther.

In a few minutes Paka came after me. I had sat down on the rough planks and stared into the muddy water. *You ruined my life.* Would Paka have written a note like that?

"You're disappointed in me, aren't you, Jo? That I didn't fight back, tell the police. You believe in the police doing what's right. You don't understand."

I gathered my thoughts. "I—I'm not disappointed in you, Paka. I'm mad. You didn't trust me. If you'd have told me—"

"What would you have done? What *could* you have done?" she asked.

"I'd have told Daddy. He'd have done something. You know he would."

"Jo, we did what we thought was best at the time. You're too trusting. Until you worked at the newspaper, you were protected from the real world. What happened to me is the real world. My world. Your world is different. It always has been, it always will be." Paka sat down beside me.

Both of us stared at the water, smooth as glass, disturbed only occasionally by a fish coming to the surface and sending an ever widening circle of ripples toward the shore.

A million thoughts bounced in my head, churned in my stomach, sending ripples farther and farther into my heart. We never really know someone as well as we think. No matter who it is, no matter how close two people are, each has secrets. Some darker, some more terrible than others. I started to cry. Paka reached out and held me tight.

"I'm so sorry, Paka. I'm so sorry," I sobbed.

"Hey, girl, it's okay. It happened a long time ago. I'm sorry I couldn't tell you."

"You didn't trust me," I sniffed, trying to control my emotions.

"No, that's not it. Don't ever think that. I just didn't want you feeling my pain."

"I feel it now. It's just as bad. I'm going to help you, Paka. I'm going to help you get through this new stuff. I wasn't there for you before, but I'm here for you now."

"I know. I know you are." She patted me on the back.

We both started to cry again. We sat there bawling like two little kids. I realized I was crying for Paka, but I was also crying for myself, for my mother and my father, for everything bad that ever happened to anyone in the whole world. And I resolved to straighten out one bad thing—the police arresting Paka for murder—if there was any possible way to do so.

CHAPTER 10

The phone was ringing when Paka and I came back into the house. I blew my nose, took a deep breath, and answered. I wasn't all that surprised to hear Olen Judd's voice. They had said they'd call before they left for home.

"The police won't let us leave town, Jo. How about you and Paka meet us for dinner tonight?" Olen's statement gave me a little information. Dods had told Paka not to leave town—as if she would. But maybe they'd told everyone at the reunion to be available for questioning again. Unless—unless Olen Judd had a connection to Hank Meeler that I didn't know about.

"Dinner with Judds?" I scribbled on a notepad by the phone and handed it to Paka.

She wiped her eyes and nodded. Good. I'd ask Olen why he was stuck in Hot Springs for longer than he'd planned.

"Sure, Olen. We'll meet you. How about some catfish at Jernigan's? It's in the Downtowner on Central. You can walk up there from the Arlington."

We agreed on five-thirty. I looked at Paka. Her face was in a pout. "What? Maybe neither of us feel like going out, but let's go anyway."

"I hoped they'd invite us to eat at the Arlington Hotel," she explained.

I smiled. "Jernigan's has better catfish. The Arlington is expensive. We can't just assume they're buying."

"I'm going home for a shower and fresh clothes." Paka picked up the packet of photos on the kitchen table. "Let's show these to Olen and Iva Nell."

"I'll pick you up at five," I said. "No use taking two cars up there. It's hard to park."

*   *   *

A cool shower renewed my spirits and body. I hoped I could stay awake through dinner. I dressed in a denim skirt and vest over a red and white knit top. I feared I was hooked on makeup, now that I'd seen what it could do for my image. I took the time to use the box of junk I'd bought at the beauty shop. I didn't have a taste for anything fancy. My choice of earrings was three sizes of gold and silver hoops: tiny hoops for working, medium for business out of the house, large for dress-up. I chose medium silver. This was a working dinner.

I laughed when I arrived at Paka's and she ran out to hop in the car. "You look like the Pink Panther." I could have cried for days over the secret that Paka had shared this afternoon, but I tried to put it aside for now. It appeared that Paka had done so, but she had lived with it longer than I had.

"When change is in order, I change. That makeover

lady said pink was my color." Paka held out her hand with a new coat of hot pink fingernail polish.

"Did she mean you should cover yourself in pink? Where's the pink bow for your hair?" I was glad that Paka felt good enough to dress up. I'd be depressed as hell if the police suspected me of murder. Or at the idea that I could be arrested and go to jail at any minute. In spite of all her wisecracking, Paka is a lot more positive than I am. And she certainly has a lot more faith in herself and in God, if not others.

Paka patted the haystack hairdo she'd been able to reproduce. "I decided a bow might be a little too much. I don't want to make Olen think I'm trying to get in the movies."

I sighed. Paka had on hot pink tights and a paler pink knit top. A tight belt reminded me that she was thin. No matter what she ate, she didn't gain weight. If I even looked at deep-fried catfish and french fries, I put on two pounds. I was going for three pounds tonight with pecan pie.

Olen and Iva Nell had arrived before us and were enjoying a mixed drink. They were such a perfect couple that a tiny bit of envy slipped out. No matter how many times I said I didn't want to get married, a little gremlin whispered, "But someone to love you would be frosting on the cake." Work could take up ninety-five percent of my life. I could spare five percent of my time for romance if it happened.

Olen stood up and shook our hands. "Jo and Paka, you look—" He stared at Paka. "Lovely. A vision in pink." He grinned.

Paka sniffed and held herself a little straighter. "Some people know nothing about fashion, do they, Iva Nell?"

Iva Nell grinned too. "Olen usually pays no attention to what women wear unless they're on the big screen.

You have his attention."

"Told you," I whispered and stuck an elbow in Paka's ribs as we sat down opposite the Judds.

She ignored me. "So tell us, Olen," she said, "how long have you been a fan of Hank Meeler's?"

"You two making like detectives?" Olen asked and sipped his drink.

"As long as we're putting together stories for the newspaper, we thought we'd see what we could find out." I was surprised that Paka asked Olen about Hank, but I was glad too. I didn't have to think of a way to be polite. Paka didn't hold much with being polite.

Olen played with the stir stick in his drink. "I admit I did hate Hank when we were in high school. He went out of his way to make jokes about me. The year I had to take PE was a nightmare. One day, he and his friends stuffed me in a locker—the supply locker if you're wondering how that was possible. I missed all of sixth period. Another time he and his buddies gathered around to watch me shower. Never said a word, just watched. And someone was always hitting me with a wet towel."

"Well, you were a wimp," Iva Nell teased. She wrapped both arms around one of Olen's to soften her teasing. "You should have used your brainpower to get back at them."

"Didn't seem worth my time. I knew I was a nerd. I felt fine about not playing football or any other sport. But Hank seemed to have a problem with it."

"Why do you think Hank chose you to pick on?" I asked, ordering a glass of iced tea. "Did he pick on anyone else?"

"Probably. I tried to ignore him, but ignoring Hank Meeler and half the football team was difficult." Olen studied his empty glass. "You two have any ideas about who might have hated him more than I did? Who might have hated him enough to kill him?"

I avoided looking at Paka and thought about my list of suspects. *You ruined my life.* I remembered the note. Unless there was more to Olen's story of the past, Hank didn't appear to have ruined Olen's life.

"Did you ever go out with Hank, Iva Nell?" I turned the spotlight on her.

"No way. I always had my eye on Olen. Took him awhile to know it, though."

"How did you two get together?" Paka asked as she played with her salad.

"I followed Olen to California. Got a job on the set of his first movie."

"But you didn't get paid much." Olen laughed.

"I had to live at the Y and eat day-old bread. It's not bad with cheap peanut butter. I took my first paycheck and got a makeover. Took me six months to finish paying for it. But it paid off. Olen came up to me the one time he took his eye off the filming and said—" She started to laugh.

Olen finished her story. "I said, 'You look familiar. Do I know you?' I'm sure she wanted to kill me."

Bad choice of words, Olen. I looked at Iva Nell. "And what did she say?"

"She said she sat behind me in all my classes at Hot Springs High School. Goes to show you, you have to sit beside or in front of someone to catch his eye."

"I didn't want to be pushy, and I was too shy to speak to him," Iva Nell explained.

"Good grief. We were all nerds." Paka laughed and reached eagerly for the plate of deep-fried catfish that the waitress handed her.

"Most people are really insecure when they're in high school." Olen tasted the wine he'd ordered and then poured glasses for everyone. "I was lucky to already be interested in film. I put up with school. Then when I wasn't reading, I was in the movie theater or in front of my VCR looking at old movies."

"You were strong enough not to care what someone else thought of you." I understood what Olen was saying. "I spent most of my time writing or going with Paka to take photos."

"The people who felt they had to be popular were probably the most miserable," Iva Nell said as she sipped her wine. She looked as if she never ate more than a few bites of food at meals.

"You two want to look at photos?" Paka pulled out a packet from her huge purse and fanned them on the table. "I got a cute one of you. But we're looking for clues in the pictures. You might see something we missed."

I grabbed the one that slid nearest me. "I guess J.D. Stroud could have been invited by someone, a woman. But I'm still surprised to see he was at the party. Olen, would a bookie kill a client who owed him a lot of money?"

"That doesn't make sense, Jo." Olen pursed his lips and sipped his wine as he looked at each photo in turn. "Then he'd never get his money back."

"How would you bet on horses out of the Hot Springs season?" I asked.

"Easy, a bookie knows the races running all over the country. Knows the odds. He'll take your bet on any of them," Olen explained.

"I heard that Hank had money problems. In fact, I think he was desperate for money." I could reveal that fact without betraying Corki. It would come out sooner or later.

"Who's this? And why does she have a coat on?" Olen pointed to Betty Sue Trotter.

I took the photo and looked closer. Betty Sue was wearing a lightweight coat and white gloves. "That's Betty Sue Biltmore, now Trotter. She married Quincy Trotter. Lots of people wore light wraps because of the rain earlier. I had a shawl, but I left it in the car. Corki said she sent Hank to get her coat. She was going home early. I guess Betty Sue was leaving too. She seemed tired when I talked to her."

"Everyone gets excited about the weather cooling off. I'm always eager to get out my jackets." Paka looked at other photos. "Whoa, look at this. I didn't see Venice there when I took this picture. Wonder if Corki noticed."

I took the picture that Paka held out. Venice Harwood stood slightly behind Hank Meeler and Corki. Anyone who saw the way she was looking at Hank would know they had a thing going.

"You think Corki found out Venice was Hank's mistress and killed him herself?" I asked. I didn't want to think that Corki killed Hank, but I realized it was a possibility. I couldn't let feeling sorry for her cloud my thinking or take her off my suspect list. Could she really have isolated herself so much from Hank and his business that she didn't know their financial situation?

Paka yawned. "Not me, girl. If I was Corki, I'd have killed Venice. That would sure have put the fear of God into old Hank."

"You two have found out a lot about Hank's affairs, haven't you?" Olen looked at each photo carefully. "Who's this?"

I looked at the picture Olen held out. "That's a jockey named Eddie Harwood. He's Venice's husband."

"He doesn't look any too fond of Hank Meeler in this photo," Olen noticed.

I was glad Paka had brought the photos. Olen was used to looking at visual images. Paka had captured Hank buying drinks. Eddie sat at the bar, staring at Hank, murder in his eyes. Did he carry out that murder as soon as he saw an opportunity?

I took my notebook out of my purse. "This case is like one of Bumpa's jigsaw puzzles. There are too many pieces cropping up all at once. To keep them straight, I'm going to have to write them down."

"Just like jolly Old Saint Nick." Paka started to sing a Christmas song in August. "You're making a list and checking it twice."

"Yeah," I said. "Gonna find out who's been naughty or nice."

It felt good to laugh. Murder among friends was out of season. My list of who might have been naughty enough to kill Hank Meeler was getting awfully long.

I shared another piece of information that I hoped Corki had already given the police. Would they keep it secret? Should I forget I'd seen it? I gambled on Olen and Iva Nell not being gossips. "Corki Meeler showed me a note Hank had gotten. He'd hid it in a dresser drawer."

Paka looked at me. She seemed upset—that Corki found the note or that I hadn't told her? I didn't think Paka would send anyone a threatening note. She'd threaten Hank to his face. "You didn't tell me that, Jo. What did the note say?" she asked.

"Someone said Hank had ruined his or her life. The note writer threatened Hank."

"Someone warned Hank he or she was going to kill him?" Olen asked. He seemed surprised.

I nodded and kept eating. The fish was sinfully good.

"*Cherchez la femme*," Iva Nell said softly.

"What's that mean?" Paka asked. "Speak English."

"Look for the woman. I think a woman would send a note like that."

Olen disagreed. "I don't think you can say only women do this, only men do that. I've seen both sexes do crazy things."

"But you live in Hollywood. Isn't everyone crazy there?" I lightened the conversation a little once I'd done what I meant to do. I wanted to see how Olen and Iva Nell reacted to the note. Somehow I didn't think either of them had sent it. But I agreed with Olen. Anyone, under stress or certain circumstances, is capable of doing almost anything. Even killing someone.

One could never solve a mystery by guessing. I made a mental note to go talk to Ernie Dodswell tomorrow. I'd see what he would tell me about his investigation. Maybe we could trade information.

The rest of the evening, I'd put aside my investigation and Paka's problems, and enjoy hearing Olen tell us about some of the crazy people he worked with in Hollywood. Crazy people I went to high school with could wait a few hours.

CHAPTER 11

I phoned Ernie Dodswell first thing the next morning. "Meet me at Annie's, Dods. I'll buy you a donut."

"What's with cops and donuts? I want ham and eggs, hash browns, a short stack."

"It's your waistline. Whatever, I'm buying."

"Breakfast."

I shrugged, as if he could see me. I wasn't offering a bribe. He knew that. "Breakfast," I said. And whatever else I could worm out of him. I knew he was a very professional cop, but maybe we could trade information.

Paka had come home with me, but she was still asleep. She was going to be mad because I kept going off without her, but I didn't think Dods would share any tidbits about the murder with her. He might let something slip if he and I seemed to be just visiting.

True to his word, Dods ordered the biggest breakfast on the menu.

I ordered a bagel and cream cheese and grinned at Dods. He grinned back. He was cute, but I kept my emotions behind barbed wire. I sure didn't want to get involved with a cop. "Off the record, Dods, do you have any theories about who killed Hank Meeler?" I decided against fishing and got straight to the point.

"Jo, there were over a hundred people at that party. Any one of them could have shot Meeler."

I could have shouted when Dods said that. I hoped it meant that Paka's chances of being arrested were a hundred to one. It meant he hadn't just decided Paka killed Meeler and stopped looking for other possibilities. I'd steer him even farther away from Paka.

"Aren't most murders committed by someone close to the victim?"

"So you think Corki Meeler did it?" Dods asked.

"Not necessarily that close. I guess she could have, but I doubt it. She had a lot of good reasons, it turns out. He had the business on the verge of bankruptcy, partly from gambling on the horses. He was cheating on her with Venice Harwood. She admits they weren't as close as they once were. But I don't think she knew all of this before Hank was killed."

Dods kept chewing and sipping coffee and shoving in more food.

"Would you like dessert?" I asked when there was only a scrap of toast left, which he used to mop up egg yolk.

"What do you think they have? Pie sounds good." He motioned for the waitress. She had been watching him and got to our booth in a nano-second. "Have any cherry pie left from last night, Sheri?"

"I saved you a piece, Dods." She smiled and left, scribbling on the ticket.

"Cops and clichés," I teased. "The way to a man's heart—"

"I haven't had much sleep since Saturday night. That means I have to eat a lot."

"Hank Meeler cheated Ray Chronister out of a lot of money on a real estate deal." So far I was the only one giving out information. I was going to be out ten bucks and come away knowing only that Dods had a big appetite—and that the waitresses at Annie's loved him.

"Corki brought me the note she found in Meeler's drawer. She said you insisted that she give it to me. Thanks, Jo. The note puts a new spin on the case. Someone planned to kill Meeler. It wasn't just a spur of the moment decision—an accidental murder."

"Are some murders accidents?" I asked.

"Sure. Two people get in a fight. A weapon is handy. One shoots the other in the heat of anger. There's hot anger and cold anger. Meeler was killed because of cold anger, don't you think?" A huge slab of cherry pie and more coffee made Dods's eyes light up. "Thanks, Sheri."

I thought out loud. "Chronister was probably angry when Meeler sold his property for a huge profit. He's had time to think about the deal—"

"And get more angry, cold anger, since it's inside, not in the heat of the moment."

I nodded. "Anilee Mowdy knew Hank was running the business into the ground. Maybe killing him was the only way she knew to stop him. He was ruining her life and ruining the business they'd built slowly over ten years."

"Sometimes living with a man for ten years can build an anger you aren't even aware of until it erupts. Corki loved Hank, but she saw him slipping away from her."

"If Venice Harwood wanted Hank to leave Corki and he wouldn't—If she wanted more than stolen time with him—" I tapped my spoon on the tablecloth while I ticked off my list.

"You're guessing, aren't you?" Dods asked. "What about the photos Paka took? I'd like to see all of them. There might be something there."

"Paka's bringing them to the station, if she hasn't already done so. My instincts keep telling me that a woman killed Hank. I'm going to go talk to Betty Sue Trotter this afternoon."

"Why Betty Sue?" Dods wanted to know.

"She dated Hank in high school. Maybe she can't forget that he dumped her for Corki. Ten years is long enough for anger to turn into an iceberg."

"My wife dumped me for another guy. I haven't considered shooting her. I told her that being married to a cop would be hard. I still get angry about her leaving me sometimes, but I understand," Dods said.

"That's the difference. You understand why she left. She probably spent all day cooking. You scarfed up the food without even saying thank you."

"Thanks for breakfast, Jo," he laughed, "even though it was a bribe. You thought I'd tell you all my secrets, didn't you?"

"I hoped I'd learn something."

"The gun that killed Meeler was small—small enough to fit in a purse, a pocket, a camera case—32 caliber, a piss-off weapon."

"Why is it called a piss-off gun?" I had to ask.

"Let's say you're assaulted. You point the gun at a guy, he laughs. Makes him angry more than protecting you. We chauvinistic men think it's more often a woman's gun, but there are shooters and collectors who love them. You have to know what you're doing to kill someone with a 32. Where to point it. Otherwise the victim is wounded but not dead. The gun makes a pretty loud pop, but people thought they were hearing champagne corks blowing off. A sound you might expect at a big party. The gun would have left powder burns on the murderer's hand."

I didn't remind him that he'd tested Paka's hands. "What if the killer wore gloves?"

"Powder on the gloves. No fingerprints. He could have thrown the gloves away, but we searched all the trash cans. The serial number on the gun was filed off, again saying this was planned. A 32 is registered to Paka. Does she know where her gun is?"

"I'd think so. You'll have to ask her." I realized that if Dods found out about Meeler raping Paka, he'd have his cold anger. Even more reason to arrest her. "Dods—"

"Don't say it. I let Paka go home with you, but she's still my number one suspect. I'm being pressured to arrest someone, Jo."

"You can't arrest Paka just because you need to please the public or your supervisors," I reasoned.

"You can believe she'd never kill anyone, Jo. You can think you know her, but people are full of surprises. And under certain circumstances—Well, let's just say anyone is capable of murder if provoked to the point of losing control."

I couldn't argue with Dods. I thought I knew everything about Paka. Now I knew I didn't. Two days ago, I'd have sworn she'd never deliberately kill anyone. Now I wasn't even sure about that. I bit my lip, feeling I'd gone backwards this morning. I hadn't learned a thing except that nothing in life is ever sure. I covered my bad feelings with anger.

"I've told you everything I know about this case, Dods. You've given me nothing."

"I gave you the check. I thought this was social. You only wanted to buy me breakfast." He grinned and I wanted to sock him, even if he was in uniform.

"How much jail time would I get for assaulting a cop?" I asked.

"Too long." He kept smiling and looked at his watch. "Catch you later."

I grabbed the check, paid, left Sheri a hefty tip—she had kept Dods happy—and hurried back out to my car. I'd go swim until hot anger—well, I should say frustration—had cooled. I should have known better than to think Dods would talk.

After a swim, I'd wake up Paka, make a plan for the day, and maybe even see if I could make something happen. I used to hunt pheasants with my dad. We didn't sit around waiting for the birds to step out of the brush. We sent a bird dog in to flush the birds and make them fly.

I needed to think about who was on my short list of likely suspects. What might flush out a murderer? How much of a risk would that be to me?

Watch your back, Jolene.

CHAPTER 12

"Where did you sneak off to so early?" Paka said in an accusing voice when I returned from a swim that got rid of a lot of junk and energized me for action. She had planned to get up early and work in the darkroom.

"I *sneaked* off to breakfast with Ernie Dodswell, if you have to know. I thought you were getting up early to work." When had Paka bought a pink chenille bathrobe? I resigned myself to a pink pussycat from now on. She was hooked.

"Plans change. I was tired." She stretched, yawned, and raised her eyebrows. "Dods?"

"It was a business breakfast." I grabbed a bottle of water out of the fridge and sat down at the breakfast table with her.

"Business? Okay, if you say so. Learn anything?"

"No. I spent ten bucks to learn how much Dods eats, as if I didn't already know. And he wanted to know if

73

you knew where your gun was. Said Meeker was killed with a 32 and you have a 32."

"My gun is where I left it. I checked when I went home yesterday."

"Good. He also wants to see all your photographs."

"Why doesn't he look at the set I left at the police station?"

"Good question." I grinned. "Guess he slipped up there."

"Don't you get involved with a cop, girl, you hear?" Paka warned.

"I know better. You don't have to warn me." I stared at my water. "Paka, when you argued with Hank about Bessie's mortgage, did he—? What did he—?"

"He didn't remember—he didn't even know me, Jo. Did you think he'd apologize?"

"No, I guess not." I reached up and pulled the wall phone receiver down to my level.

"Who are you calling?" Paka asked.

"Everyone." I dialed Corki's number first and rubbed my hair with a towel while I waited. Her message machine picked up. "Corki, Jo here. Paka and I have been looking at the photos she took at the reunion. We've found something I think you'd find interesting in one of them. Call me when you get home and I'll bring it over for you to see." I hung up.

Paka's eyebrows formed arches over eyes that were huge with curiosity. "What? What did we find?"

"I don't know. Start looking." I reached for the packet that she had set on the divider between the kitchen and the dining area last night. I handed them to her as I dialed again.

"Ray, Jo here. No, no, I haven't decided to sell my place. I told you I have no plan to move, so start looking for another spot. What I did want to tell you is that I have something strange on one of the photos Paka took that I thought might interest you. It's one that she just developed, so the police haven't seen it." I gave Ray a chance to say something, but he didn't. "Why don't you come over tomorrow about four in the afternoon and take a look." I took his silence as a yes and hung up. Was he not interested or was he too concerned to speak?

"Girl, what are you doing?" Paka asked.

"Baiting the hook. The reason I like fishing so much is that you never know what might be on your line." I had a bunch of mixed metaphors going here, but flushing birds, baiting fish—all would get the same result. If I held out the bait to the right person.

I made a similar phone call to Venice Harwood, leaving a message on her machine too. Maybe Eddie would also listen. Then, what the heck, I called J.D. Stroud. He had a machine. It was easier to leave my message, I found. I didn't want anyone asking too many questions, since I didn't have any answers. Anilee Mowdy was out, probably showing a home. I had my story polished by the time her voice mail picked up. I dialed the Arlington Hotel and left a message for Olen and Iva Nell Judd, saying Paka had developed some new pictures that they might find interesting. I had pretty much ruled them out as suspects, but as Dods said, 'People are full of surprises.'

"I think you may be fishing for trouble," Paka warned. "What are you going to show these people in my photos when they come looking?"

"I don't know. You have to help me find things. But first, I want you to go with me, out to Betty Sue Trotter's place. I got so depressed just standing by her the other night, I was ready to drink your martini. I need you to cheer up both of us if she's in the same mood."

"Did it ever occur to you to ask me if I wanted to go cheer up somebody?" Paka asked.

"No, I just assumed you hated being left behind. Didn't you suggest that when you accused me of sneaking out this morning?"

Paka took a deep breath and pulled her mouth into a thin line. Probably to keep from smiling. She spread out her photographs again and studied each carefully. I called Betty Sue and she said if we'd come right away, she'd be home.

The Trotters lived out near Lakewood School where Betty Sue's husband Quincy was a PE teacher and football coach. Lakewood used to be out in the country, but Hot Springs had grown bigger and bigger until the city merged with the rural community. A lot of wealthy people who wanted more land had built huge homes out toward the school.

"While I was at the newspaper office yesterday," I said, partly to fill the silence that filled the front seat of the Nissan, "I called Lakewood School. I found out that Betty Sue taught biology there until a year ago. They said she was taking a year's leave of absence."

"What for?" Paka came back from wherever she'd been.

"I didn't think they'd tell me, so I didn't ask. Let's ask her."

Betty Sue had given me directions to get to her house. If she had said pick out the house that looks out of place, I'd have found it. We passed a lot of mansions, homes set back into manicured, wooded land. Thick tangles of undergrowth had been cleared and replaced by green lawns that needed a riding mower to groom.

The Trotter property had been a small farm, and the small, shabby farmhouse still stood, looking as if a strong wind would send it to Tennessee. Betty Sue met us at the front door, standing in it as if she'd like to turn us away, not invite us inside.

"Can we come in and talk?" I finally asked, not willing to visit at the door.

"I guess so. Quincy is over at the school. I was gonna go out to Wal-Mart before he got home. I wanted to get me some of those little wooden TV tables they advertised."

"We can't stay long." Paka looked around, moved some magazines off a tattered couch, and sat down.

"Would you like a Coke?" Betty Sue must have decided she had no choice but to play hostess. We'd gotten in and sat down. She wasn't going to get rid of us easily.

"I would," Paka said. "Want me to help you get it?"

"Oh, no. You sit down. I'll be right back." She hurried off toward the back of the house. "I didn't really want to see the kitchen," Paka whispered.

I knew what she meant. Betty Sue wasn't the world's greatest housekeeper. Magazines were strewn all over the living room, mostly woman's magazines. *Soap Opera Digest*. Crossword puzzle books with pages open to puzzles half worked. Dust coated all the tables and lamps, and dust kittens rolled around between faded area rugs on ancient brown linoleum. I was glad to see the Coke come in a can, not a glass that might not be terribly clean. What was wrong with this woman? I didn't remember her being sloppy in high school.

Betty Sue perched on the edge of a straight-back chair and looked at us while she sipped her Coke. She didn't have on any makeup. Her dark, almost black, hair was limp and oily-looking. She set her Coke on an end table, reached up with both hands, and tucked her hair behind her ears, which made it look even worse. She had a prominent widow's peak that called attention to her high forehead. Some bangs would have helped her face. I wanted to hunt in my purse for the card the beauty operator gave me over in Little Rock. Betty Sue could use her help. She reminded me of the old photos I'd seen of pioneer or hill country women who'd worked hard and had a dozen children.

"You're not teaching anymore?" I had to say something, and quick. I found my spirits sliding off into the swamp of Betty Sue's depression.

"I stopped teaching to have children a year ago. I thought—I'd heard that sometimes stress and fatigue can keep you from getting pregnant. Quincy was okay with my not working. He makes a good salary, you know."

And she didn't spend a lot of money on her house or herself. But I didn't want to talk about her not having any children. I'd assume that was why Betty Sue was unhappy.

"You knew Hank pretty well, Betty Sue," I said. "Didn't you go with him for a year or two before he met Corki?"

"Two years. I thought it was going to be forever. And it would have if Corki hadn't showed up. She was just so pretty." Betty Sue stared at her Coke can, drew lines on the moisture forming on the outside.

"But you were really cute." Paka smiled at Betty Sue. "I always thought you were cute. I was envious, because I was such a giant. I doubt I was even cute the day I was born." Paka was sincere, not making something up to make Betty Sue feel better.

"Maybe I was. But cute wasn't good enough once Hank saw Corki."

"Were you angry when he dropped you for Corki?" I asked.

"Of course I was, Jo. Wouldn't you be?" Her brown eyes flashed.

"For a while. You aren't still mad at Hank, are you?" Cold anger, that's what I was looking for. Had I found it?

"He's dead. No use being mad at a dead man." Her voice was flat, dead too.

"Oh, geez, Paka," I said suddenly, with great energy in my voice. "You let me forget that photo I wanted to show Betty Sue."

Paka's face said, 'I did?' and 'What are you talking about?'

"What photo?" Betty Sue asked. "I hope it wasn't of me. I don't like having my picture taken." She swiped shoulder-length hair behind her ears again.

"It was. Paka took several photos of everyone who was at the party. But this one she just developed. It wasn't in the batch we gave the police. I just wanted to ask you about something in the photo, the way you were looking at Hank."

Paka helped me bait this hook. "I think I must have taken that picture a short time before Hank was shot."

"I just needed you to explain something to me," I added.

"What?" Betty Sue asked.

"Well, you'd have to see it. Maybe we can come back sometime tomorrow. Unless you're going to be in town. I could meet you someplace, or you could come out to the house. I live on the lake, remember?"

"I know where you live. We had a party out there one time. But I don't know why—"

"It's probably nothing. I was just curious." I left the juicy worm of a photograph hanging. I wasn't sure what I was going to show people if they all showed up at my place to see what I was talking about. My plan was that only Hank Meeler's killer would be worried enough to come to look at a photo that might reveal his identity.

I looked at Paka. She read my mind and stood up. "Well, we've got to go, girl. We're keeping you from your shopping, and I want to get back to my darkroom. I have a lot of film to develop yet. No telling what I'll find. Sometimes I think I don't see a place—except through the eye of a camera—until I get home and look at the pictures. I'm still at the reunion out there in my darkroom."

"That must be strange." Betty Sue seemed not to know what else to say.

I left, taking the rest of my Coke with me. In the car, I took another big swig. "God, I had to get out of there. That woman is in trouble. I wanted to tell her to see a doctor or a psychiatrist or get some help someplace."

"Or a makeover. She *was* really cute. I wasn't just saying that." Paka was concerned too.

"I don't think a haircut and some makeup is going to do it for her," I said as I headed back to town. "Let's stop and get some McClard's barbeque to go with our Cokes, Paka. We'll take Bumpa some in case he never got there last night. If I get my appetite back by the time we drive a few miles." I shook my head, trying to get rid of the negative atmosphere of Betty Sue's home and her personality.

"I do have a lot of film to develop," Paka said. "You might not be lying to all these people. We may still find some clues in my photos. I'll eat and go to work. You keep exercising your little gray cells. I'd laugh if we solved this crime before Mr. Hotshot Ernie Dodswell."

I was glad Paka didn't say before Dods came to arrest her. And I'd save my laughter till later. I just hoped I hadn't opened the door to trouble by telling my short list of suspects that I had a clue that might lead us to the murderer.

CHAPTER
13

"Jo—" Paka paused and looked out the car window. When she calls me Jo instead of girl or some insulting tag, I know she's going to say something serious. I thought I knew what it was.

"Jo, I don't like the idea of your risking your life for me. Inviting all those people out to the lake, hoping you'll lure the murderer out there. What if you do? He's already killed Hank. He wouldn't hesitate to kill you or me."

"Yeah, I figure old Betty Sue will come after both of us." I tried to make a joke of baiting a hook for our suspects who might have killed Hank Meeler.

"Yeah, both of us, with a dust mop and a broom. I'll bet that place hasn't been cleaned since last Christmas." Paka was ready to laugh again.

"Or longer," I said. "And if she wants to get pregnant, she's going to have to fix herself up a little for the man Quincy."

"Yo, Quincy, my man, send your wife over to Little Rock for a makeover. Look what it did for the two of us beautiful women," Paka laughed.

Then Paka got serious again. I picked up on a whole carload of serious vibes. I jumped in before Paka said anything. "I can't just let them send you away, Paka, for a crime you didn't commit. What would I do without you? You're half my team. And remember that life *is* a team sport."

"Who said that?" she asked.

"I did. Occasionally I write some awesome words. But I can't, I don't even want to try to sell stories without your photos."

"Okay, just as long as you admit that you are nothing without me. Even if you wrote up my story for the *National Enquirer*, it wouldn't sell without my pictures."

"I admit it. I'll work it up in needlepoint," I joked.

"Tonight?"

"Sure. While you're developing photos."

End of serious session. I breathed a sigh of relief and took a big swallow of my Coke. There was a lot of truth in what I said. I don't know how well my writing would sell on its own, but it didn't matter. I didn't want to work without Paka.

We phoned ahead for our barbeque order, then swung by McClard's and picked it up. Paka ran inside. "Did you get fries?" I asked when she returned with a bag that filled the car with spicy smells.

"Of course. Drive fast so all this doesn't get cold."

We shared our dinner with Bumpa. Then Paka left to go into her darkroom and develop the rest of her film. I headed back to my computer to write another story for the newspaper.

I didn't have much, if any, new information, so it took me a long time to make up something that Ed the Editor would go for. I left the file open. Maybe Paka would have some new photos that would inspire me and add to what I'd written.

I realized too that Anilee Mowdy would have a list of everyone who attended the party. I'd call her in the morning. I might be missing someone else who hated Hank Meeler. I'd gone for the obvious people first. I might need to make my short list a little longer.

I glanced at my watch. Good Lord, it was past midnight. Surely Paka wasn't still bent over a pan of print solution or staring at photos hung up to dry. I hadn't heard her come in, and she would have come into my office when she did. She'd have told me what she found, if anything, or that she was going to bed, calling it a night.

I laughed. I'd bet she had fallen asleep. There was an old couch in the darkroom. Sometimes all Paka had to do was sit down and she'd be asleep. I'd found her snoozing on the job more than once.

I stomped out the back door, turning back to grab a flashlight. The yard lights weren't on. They didn't come on when I flipped the switch beside the door. Did all the bulbs burn out at once?

"Okay, Pussycat, I need help with this story." I'd admit it again. "I need some inspiration from your photographs." I could mention some other people who were at the reunion. Tell what they were doing ten years later. Olen Judd might be the most successful, but he wasn't the only successful graduate of our class. If I nosed around enough, I could find some more stories instead of rehashing the murder scene. Readers had that memorized.

The dogs had heard me from their garage beds. They

caught up as I headed down the path to the boathouse. Shena yawned.

"Sorry to have bothered you, Shena," I said. "You didn't have to get up and come out here with me."

Sui looked at me and smiled. Yes we did, he seemed to say. You might find out how useless we are and fire us from our watchdog positions.

I entered the boathouse from the dock. Then I made my way through the junk to the room built across the back for Paka's darkroom. I turned off my light and knocked, even though opening the door at night wouldn't ruin any photos. "Paka?"

No answer. Yep, she was asleep. I cracked the door and peeked in. Red lights cast an eerie glow over the tables and pans of chemicals. Over the clothesline were only a couple of photos dangled to dry. A late-night radio station that played mostly blues filled the room with a mellow beat. A chair was turned on its side. Shelves of supplies had been dumped out. Photos littered the floor as if someone had looked at each and tossed it aside.

"Paka?" Where was she? My heart pounded against my rib cage and my stomach flipped over. My eyes traveled from the work area to the couch in the corner, then to the floor in front of the couch. "Paka!"

Even in the semi-darkness, I could see that Paka wasn't asleep. Her left arm rested under her body in a strange position. And across her forehead was an ugly gash, made even more horrible by the pool of blood beneath her head.

Chapter 14

Paka groaned and started to come to. She tried to get up.

"Thank God you're alive, but don't move."

"What hit me?"

"You didn't see who did this?" I asked.

"What? Hit me? No, I didn't see him."

"Okay, just stay there, lying down. I'll call Bumpa and an ambulance. You may have a concussion." I also didn't want Paka to see the mess her darkroom was in. She'd had enough shock.

The dogs started barking at the same time I heard a noise. A bouncing, hollow thud, like an oar hitting the concrete floor in the boathouse.

I left Paka, hoping she'd stay put, and shined my light around. Whoever had hit Paka and ransacked the dark room was still in the boathouse, or had been.

Fortunately, I shined my light around the room before I took off running. No wonder the dogs were barking. A huge rattler coiled, head weaving, tongue flicking in and out, testing the air for smells and the warmth of a body.

I froze, my light on the snake. "Back Shena, Sui, get back. Please don't attack."

The oar. I knew approximately where it should be. Quickly, I swept the wall with the light. Then I stepped sideways and grabbed the wooden canoe paddle that had made the noise hitting the floor. Someone had bumped it, knocking it down, warning me.

In seconds, I had grabbed up the paddle and spot-lighted the rattlesnake again. "Get back, Shena," I repeated, moving a few inches closer to the coiled threat. If the dogs moved away from it, the snake might uncoil and glide away. Most snakes aren't aggressive. They will try to escape an enemy once they feel it's safe.

This one definitely didn't feel safe. I'd have to take a chance. I slid my foot inches closer, raised the paddle with my right hand, and kept the snake in the light with my left. Inches closer, stop, aim. I had to hit the snake's head dead center with one blow. I wouldn't have time for a second swing before it struck. I had seen the results of rattlesnake bites, but I'd never been bit myself. This wasn't a good time for a first experience.

The snake's tongue continued to explore the air. I tightened my focus and my grip on both paddle and flashlight. Aimed. Prayed. Swung.

Thud! I felt the soft body all the way up the paddle and into my arm. Into my mind. But my aim was true. I had paddle-chopped the snake squarely across its diamond-shaped head. In fact, I had practically severed the head from the body.

"Sorry," I said. Even in the life-threatening situation, I knew the snake was innocent. The only way the rattler could have gotten into the boathouse in the minutes since I first walked through was via person. Someone had dropped the snake, hoping if I gave chase, I'd either be slowed or stopped by dealing with it. I was slowed, but not stopped.

Throwing the paddle aside, I yelled for Bumpa to come and help Paka. I took off running out of the boathouse, up the path toward the house. I stopped. Listened. A few seconds later and I wouldn't have heard the footsteps crunching twigs and pinecones on the path into the woods.

"Gotcha." I picked up my speed and dashed off into the darkness. My light bobbed up and down as I ran, but I knew the path. I had walked it many a night with the dogs. They took off behind me, thinking this was a new midnight game we were playing. Oh boy, fun.

Oh boy, disaster. Who was I following? Was I going to end up lying on the trail like Paka was lying on the darkroom floor? I pulled up and stopped for a second. Heard nothing.

For some reason, both dogs stopped behind me. Silence. The person I was chasing had either gotten away or stopped too. I waited. He waited. The woods waited. Just as a cricket felt it was safe to chirp again, I heard the gasp.

Footsteps continued, not far ahead of me.

I held my breath. I ran, picking up speed.

Then, *smack!* I couldn't stop in time. I flattened the person I was chasing and three bodies went down together.

CHAPTER 15

I recovered first. "Ray! Ray Chronister, it was you!"

Chronister held his hand in front of his face as I shined the light directly into his eyes. "Damn it, Jo, get that light out of my eyes."

But who? Someone under me groaned. I shined the light on the third body. "Betty Sue Trotter? What are you doing here?"

"Help. I need help, Jo. That—that damn snake." Betty Sue rolled up her pants leg to expose a set of red marks and a quickly swelling leg.

"You mean it wasn't Ray? You left that snake in the boathouse? You hit Paka, ransacked the dark room, and left Paka to die?" I was babbling.

"She wasn't dead."

My brain was really slow. "You—you murdered Hank Meeler? You came out to see what evidence Paka had uncovered in her photos that would tell us who the killer was?"

She tried to get up. I held her down. "Then what are you doing out here in the woods, Ray?" I was going to get some answers before I went anyplace.

"That call, Jo. After I thought about it, I realized that I wasn't the only one you called. And if you called the killer— Well, I was worried about you. I came out here to help you."

"At midnight?"

"I couldn't sleep. The more I worried, the more wide awake I got. Finally, I decided to get in my car, drive out here, and check on you. Good thing I did."

I kept looking at him there in the shadows until he spoke again.

"I know you don't want me to, Jo, but I do care about you. I knew if you called everyone you suspected of murdering Hank Meeler, the killer might come out here. I saw Betty Sue take off into the woods. I didn't know who she was, but I knew where the path came out on the road. I hurried back and took the path from the opposite direction. You know the rest."

We had made a killer sandwich of Betty Sue. The thought slipped out before I could think how ridiculous it sounded, but it was true. We smacked Betty Sue between us. She groaned again, and I focused my light on her, still on the ground.

I knew what was happening. The rattler poison was shooting through her body. Adrenaline, plus her running, had speeded up circulation of the venom. Forget why she was here, what she had done. I had to get her to the hospital.

"Help me, Ray. She doesn't need to walk anymore." I pulled Betty Sue to her feet.

Ray elbowed me aside and picked her up. I could hear his huffing and puffing as he walked ahead of me on the trail back to the house. He was out of shape. I hoped he could do this. Imagine his coming out to rescue me. Despite the circumstances, I smiled and shook my head, shining a spot of light ahead of him. Some hero.

The dogs bounced and trotted on the trail, tails high like flags leading a parade. When we came into the yard, I gasped. All the lights strung down toward the lake were on. Every light in the house glared. Two police cars edged the road, lights spinning and flashing.

Ray carried Betty Sue around to the front and dumped her onto the bench in the front yard. She buried her head into her chest and hugged her arms tight around her.

"Am I having a party?" I asked, for lack of anything else to say in response to all the chaos.

Bumpa supported Paka by her good arm. She leaned on him and held a rag to her head. Despite my warnings she had gotten up off the floor and walked to the house.

Dods dashed out of the house. "Jo, thank God, there you are. Are you all right?" He looked at me, Ray, Betty Sue, and then his eyes came back to me.

Anilee Mowdy and Corki Meeler walked out of my wide-open front door. Corki spoke first. "Jo, what's going on?" She looked as if she hadn't slept since the murder, but she had on her makeup and a smart-looking pants suit, as did Anilee Mowdy.

"What are you two doing out here?" My brain swirled. Was everyone I had called here?

"I couldn't sleep. I called Anilee," Corki said. "We decided we wanted to find out what you had found out—what photo you had that revealed Hank's killer."

"Did I say that?"

"You said you had photos that gave you the evidence you needed to solve this crime."

I didn't remember using any of those exact words. Corki and Anilee had taken what I *had* said and added on what they wanted me to have found.

"That was a stupid thing to have done, Jolene Allen." Dods had the official word on my baiting the hook for the killer. And he was right, but I'd never admit it.

"It worked, didn't it?" I held back a grin.

Paka filled in what I couldn't say. "Yeah, it almost got me killed." Her voice was strong, and she was thinking up insults and smart remarks, so I knew she'd be all right. I felt a sigh of relief fill me, and my legs turned to mush. I sank down onto the bench beside Betty Sue.

"We need to get Paka and Betty Sue to the hospital," I said. "Betty Sue has a rattlesnake bite that needs to be tended to. I'd like to see her live to stand trial for the murder of Hank Meeler."

"Betty Sue Trotter killed Hank?" Another suspect heard from. Venice Harwood huddled into the shoulder of her husband, the pair looking like Bobbsey Twins, being the same height. Venice looked as if she hadn't slept much lately either. Yard shadows added to the shadows under her eyes and bruised hollow cheeks. "Why?"

While we waited for Betty Sue to speak—if she would—I realized what had happened. Everyone, or almost everyone, I had called had decided to come out to the lake about the same time. No one had been able to sleep. Curiosity was alive and well for the ten-year high school veterans.

I also realized that had Betty Sue not been so violent in her attempt to see the photos, I'd have all the suspects sitting in a circle, waiting for me to point out the killer. And I would not have had an answer for them. Betty Sue showed her hand out of fear and panic, out of desperation. And, I wondered, if not out of a bit of madness. Surely she wasn't thinking in a sane way when she killed Hank.

"Why did you kill Hank, Betty Sue?" I reminded her of what we were all waiting for.

At first her words came softly; then they tumbled out and her anger built. Cold anger. "He ruined my life. Of course, I couldn't have the baby, but he could have gotten me a better doctor, not some butcher who'd ruin my chances of ever again getting pregnant."

Corki's face registered shock. "Hank got you pregnant, Betty Sue? When?"

"Before you stole him from me, that's when. Maybe if you hadn't come along, he'd have married me, and I could have had the baby. We would have survived the scandal. He would have done the right thing by me. But no, he said I had to have an abortion, that I couldn't tell anyone. He'd find a doctor to do it. He'd pay for the surgery. Surgery! The man probably wasn't even a doctor, just some sleazy pretender wanting the money."

"So because you had the abortion, the procedure left you unable to have children?" I asked it as a formal question.

Betty Sue started to cry. "Shut up, just shut up, all of you! You all looked down on me in high school. No one thought I was good enough for Hank Meeler. I couldn't stand by and watch him have four children, become rich and successful, and never pay for what he had done to me. Finally I decided to do something about it. What better place than in a room full of people he was always trying to impress? I'm glad he's dead. Glad, you hear?"

"Betty Sue needs to get to the hospital," I reminded Dods. "Did you call for an ambulance?"

Before he could answer, a siren's whine filled the woods around us and another vehicle with flashing lights stopped on the road.

"Paka—" I began.

"I'm okay," she answered. "My arm is sprained but not broken. And I have a hard head, remember? I'll go get some stitches later, Jo. I have to develop those photos all over again. We have to get a story to the newspaper in time for tomorrow's headlines."

"Ever the professional, aren't you, Paka Powell?" Olen Judd grinned at Paka. Had he and Iva Nell just arrived, or had they been standing on the sidelines listening?

"Well, Olen," I said. "Why are you here? Come to get an idea for your next film?"

"No," Iva Nell answered for them, "this story is too sad. Poor Betty Sue."

I resisted saying, poor Hank. He'd paid for his sins the hard way. Everyone here was a victim. Corki had lost a husband who probably would have come back to her, asking for forgiveness. Anilee had almost lost the business she'd worked so hard to build with Hank. I hoped she could save it. Ray Chronister had lost the life savings he'd put into his house and the property around it.

I had acted without thinking very far ahead and had almost lost my best friend and co-worker. Betty Sue could have easily killed Paka with a blow to the head. Hard head was right. I didn't stop her as she hurried back to the darkroom to get us some photos for our story.

The paramedics lifted Betty Sue onto a stretcher and wheeled the cart toward the ambulance. I walked along beside her. "Why in the world did you bring a rattlesnake out here, Betty Sue?"

"I had trapped it to take over to the school tomorrow.

I was giving a lecture on snakes to the biology class. I didn't know how I'd use it—as a distraction, to slow someone down. Damn thing bit me when I dumped it out. Hank hated snakes." She started to laugh. "I was always fascinated by them." Her laughter went on and on, becoming hysterical.

I stepped back while the two men lifted her into the back of the ambulance. Then I turned to find myself in the arms of Corki Meeler. She gave me a big hug and said, "Poor Betty Sue. Hank stepped on a lot of toes, but he was afraid of a lot more in life than snakes. I wish I'd have had more time to help him with those fears."

Compassion. So few people have enough. As long as Corki could continue thinking of others instead of herself, she'd pull out of this tragedy. I resolved to be a better friend to her than I had been in the past. Sometimes reunions are reminders—reminders of real friendship and what it takes to keep those relationships going over the years.

Sui tugged on my shirtsleeve as I stood and watched everyone leave. Reminding me of what it takes to keep him happy. "Yes, boy, you did a good job tonight. And I know you'd like a walk, but later. I have some blessings to count because my foolishness didn't get anyone else killed. And then a story to write."

Shena and Sui both whined and followed me to the house.

"Yes, come on in and help me." I shivered and held the door open until both dogs could trot into the living room—a rare treat that they wouldn't forget for months. But I needed the company. I needed the warmth of them next to me. I stroked Sui's head, sat down at my desk, and started to type. *Never go to your high school reunion.*